THE RANSOM INSTRUCTIONS

"When's the deadline?" Priest asked.

"In fifteen days," Sarah said.

"Where's the meeting?"

"He wants it brought to his stronghold."

"Well," Priest said without expression. "How many vaqueros does Braulio have?"

"I'm not sure, but at least fifty men, I'd be expecting. He's promised safe passage to whoever carries the ransom."

"Why don't you set the mayor and sheriff on him?"

"The note said not to inform them or he'd be killed."

"How'd the note first arrive? Rider in the night?"

"Yes, who hurled it over the wall affixed to a dagger."

"Give it to me."

She left the room and returned five minues later carrying a finely crafted blade. He took it and could immediately feel how much art and precision had gone into the weapon. This was the "slow knife" that Don Braulio liked to use against his enemies. . . .

TOM PICCIRILLI

Coffin Blues

LEISURE BOOKS   **L**   NEW YORK CITY

LEISURE BOOKS ®

June 2004

Published by

Dorchester Publishing Co., Inc.
200 Madison Avenue
New York, NY 10016

ISBN 0-8439-5336-5

The name "Leisure Books" and the stylized "L" with design are
trademarks of Dorchester Publishing Co., Inc.

Printed in the United States of America.

Visit us on the web at www.dorchesterpub.com.

For Bill Pronzini,
teacher and valued compadre.

And of course for Michelle,
who gives me a reason to fight the good fight.

The author would like to acknowledge several direct
and indirect influences in the writing of this novel.
I owe a debt of thanks to Ed Gorman, Dale L. Walker,
Andrew J. Fenady, Joe Lansdale, Dallas Mayr,
Robert Randisi, and Elmore Leonard.
Further recognition is due the memories
of H. A. DeRosso, Frank O'Rourke, and William Ard.

Coffin Blues

Chapter One

Priest had taken to building coffins.

He didn't know why but he seemed to have a gift for it, each smooth slat fitting perfectly together with the rest. Besides, he had to do something with the wagonload of cedar and Mexican pine that had been delivered over a month ago. The lumber was meant to go into the construction of more shelves for the store, but since Lamarr had gambled the goods money away in Tombstone, and Chicorah had burned down the whole place, there didn't appear to be anything he needed to do with the wood. So he'd taken to building coffins.

The storefront Priest currently used was next door to the millinery. All day long he'd watch the startled faces of the women peeking in, whipping their fans and spinning their parasols a little faster as they stared at Lamarr sleeping inside a box laid out on the floor. It kept Priest's mouth hiked into a grin for most of the afternoon, and he supposed that was as good a reason as any to make coffins.

Miss Henshaw, the milliner, had been around three times complaining that business had dropped off significantly since Priest had moved in. When he heard the front door open he figured she was coming around again to yell about how the ladies of Patience weren't perusing the new European summer hat collection the way they should've been. He didn't blame her. As soon as he finished up with the rest of the cedar and pine, he'd leave the Main Street boardwalk, but for the time being he had nothing else to do.

The burning breeze flung a rippling cloud of dust inside. Lamarr didn't even stir as Priest glanced over to the shop entrance.

She walked in and set right to work appraising each box. She had to stoop in order to inspect the coffins. One eye was so puffy it had sealed shut and the other wasn't much better. Her withered, dark face had been severely bruised and her bottom lip was split so badly it would probably never completely heal right.

Her name was Miz Utopia Jones Clay,

and she was a granny woman. She not only took care of the black folk in the south quarter, but prepared her brews, plasters, and applications for anyone who needed them. Once, she'd even tried to heal Gramps when he'd first started going Apache a couple of years back. She spent a long weekend hoping to cure the old man and get him white again, feeding him all kinds of foul-smelling stews and soups and sticking poultices on his forehead and up his nose. At the end of it, with Gramps sitting in her kitchen dressed in only a breechcloth and spouting Apache, she'd given Priest a long pitying stare and said, "Be easier jest to get the white man out of him. Wanna try that?"

Priest didn't. He was twenty-three and already going gray, a couple of silver-tinged curls right out in front. He had enough problems. He'd brought Gramps to the edge of town and let the old man run up to White Mountain where he lived with Chicorah's people for a couple of months at a time. Gramps was there right now. But he could handle it only so long, and then the rest of his whole white life pushed back through. When he started calling out his long-dead wife's name, Chicorah would know it was time to get him off the rez and send him back home before the old man commenced scaring the children.

Even with him lying in the box, you could tell Lamarr topped six foot two and weighed in at around two hundred thirty pounds of muscle and bone. His black skin gleamed with a light sheen of sweat. His short hair was fringed with a little white, but his skin was so smooth you'd never guess he was going on fifty.

Miz Utopia glared down at Lamarr in the coffin. She bent, cocked her head, and hunched a bit lower. "He daid?"

"Not the last time I checked."

She peered more closely at Lamarr. "You scrutinized him any in the last week or so?"

"I think he got up once yesterday around noon."

"I don't see no flies," she said, "but he gettin' a bit ripe."

"That's just his natural leaning."

She covered her nose. "Jesus is more merciful to some than others."

Priest had an empty feeling in his belly looking at Miz Utopia's beaten face, knowing that he and Lamarr were going to have to get into something. Vague distress and fear worked through him. He hadn't felt it for a few days now and, oddly enough, he'd actually missed it. The uneasiness and cold tension made him a little angry, and that was familiar and comforting, too. For the first time all week he grew calm and relaxed. One of these days he'd have to give all this some thought.

He whispered, "Lamarr," saying it the way he had to. Lamarr instantly opened his eyes and got up.

"You shouldn't tempt the good Lord like that none, Lamarr Russell," she told him. "You do and He might jest strike you daid."

"Miz Utopia," Lamarr said, easing his lips wide and showing off every white tooth in his head. "The Lord gonna strike me when He ready, no matter what I got to say about it." Lamarr kept the smile up but Priest saw the heavy ridge of muscle suddenly bulge across his neck and shoulders.

"What you two doin' buildin' coffins? Thought you was opening a dry goods store. Leastways I heard that."

"It didn't rightly take, that place," Lamarr said, trying to sound sad and doing a shoddy job of it. "Bad timing. Poor location. The competition in this here boomtown is fierce, ma'am, mighty ferocious."

Priest didn't argue the point or bring up Tombstone and the faro tables again. Chicorah had burned down the shop because he believed Gramps was possessed by holy *Ga'ns* mountain spirits and that

5

Priest must have better things to do with his life than run a store. Maybe it was true.

Miz Utopia moved closer and stepped inside the coffin. "You don't make them none too comfortable."

"It was fine for me," Lamarr told her, hoping to be helpful.

"You put a few pillows inside? I wouldn't want no damage. Maybe a nice soft sheet?"

"Sure," Priest said, thinking, *Damage?*

"Well, that'd be right nice. We all needs our rest. How much you askin'?"

The question surprised him. Priest didn't know what to say. He hadn't sold one yet and really never thought he would. "No charge."

"Competition can't be too mighty ferocious with prices like that. I give you a dollar. You put more padding and extra cushions in here? Cloth so nobody's head hits the sides?"

"Sure."

"I reckon I'll take it then. But I want this here coffin delivered."

Priest tried not to sigh. There was always something hard and wearisome lurking just around the corner. "Where?"

"The hill."

"Which hill?"

"Boot Hill." Miz Utopia sounded proud saying the name. "Dodge City. My husband

Willalee Enigma Jones Clay was hung there and buried with them other fellas way back some, and I reason if it's a good-enough resting place for him, then it'd be fine for the rest of the family, too."

"Ma'am—," Lamarr said, but that's as far as he got.

"I know. That there Boot Hill is filled with rustlers and gunfighters nowadays, but they's a time when it was where they placed the unwanted, and I's the only one ever wanted Willalee Enigma Jones Clay. And even I's didn't wants him all that much most of the time."

"Oh," Priest said. He couldn't help staring at her face, realizing that somebody had beaten this old woman who'd never done anything but try to help others. He could hear Chicorah telling him that he had a larger fate, the voice of the Apache sub-chief's son sounding as clear as if he'd just spoken from across the room.

"Why you holdin' a knife like that?" Miz Utopia asked.

Priest looked down. He wasn't holding his knife. He must've drawn it and put it back without realizing. Miz Utopia blinked twice at him with her good eye and gave herself a short nod as if she was pleased. She pulled a silver dollar from deep inside her skirts and said, "That there box is

7

mine now." Opening the door, she let the wind come sweeping back in, swirls of sage leaves working over her shoes. She wet her lips gingerly so the scabs wouldn't yank too badly, turned away, and hissed words that the scorching gusts brought right to Priest's ear. "I seen it. He hurtin' girls. Hardly more than children."

Then she was gone, and the ladies out in front of the milliner's shop were staring in again and tittering.

Lamarr still showed his teeth, as if he couldn't shut his mouth even if he wanted to, but now there was something dangerous in that beaming smile. "She got a boy by the name'a Burial who's always been trouble. Owns a saloon. Runs with one or two other like-minded fools."

"I don't suppose Burke would be willing to roust him."

"They fools but they smart enough to only rob other black folk in the south quarter and cause no white man distress. Sheriff Burke don't much mind them kind of nefarious doings."

"But we, being good citizens, mind such doings greatly."

Crimson sunlight angled in through the front window, casting fat wriggling shadows across the coffins. "That boy raised a hand to his own mama. The Bible got a whole lot of vengeful, wrathful things to say about that."

"So I hear tell."

"The Lord will surely take care of him, it's true, but baby Jesus, he remarkably busy saving souls all over the land."

"Think he's ever passed through Patience?"

"Maybe he's here right now," Lamarr offered, "whisperin' in my left ear."

"I think I might hear him, too," Priest said.

He glanced down again and saw the knife in his hand.

He'd have to keep a hold of himself tonight.

Coloreds weren't much welcome north of Main Street. They weren't welcome south of Main Street, either, but they had to stay someplace, and the five or six square blocks behind the livery were considered the black quarter.

Priest wasn't sure if it worked the other way around. He'd lived in Patience all his life but had never stepped foot in the black quarter, and he kept wondering if someone might beat the hell out of him here for just being white and so damn ignorant.

They drove the buckboard with Miz Utopia Jones Clay's comfortable coffin in back. Lamarr had stopped off at his shack and put in a pillow and some old blankets. He figured on what Priest was thinking and let out a low rolling chuckle that made Priest's eyebrows itch.

You could get laughed at for anything, but especially for your own willful stupidity. It reminded Priest of how oblivious he could be to the world on occasion, how little he knew about the things he should be well acquainted with by now.

Lamarr tried to offer insight and experience where he could. He'd been a slave prior to strangling the Georgian plantation master, as well as a runaway and a Union soldier for a couple of years after that before heading west looking for his white daddy, Septemus Hart. Septemus owned most of Patience and he and Lamarr kept a running game going on, jabbing at one another with threats and insults, just waiting for the right moment when they might finish each other off. The fact was, Lamarr couldn't kill the old man until Septemus admitted aloud to being Lamarr's daddy, and Septemus just didn't seem like he was ever going to oblige him.

"This the home of the free, or ain't you heard?" Lamarr said. "You ain't gotta worry about crossing this street, or the next, or any in town or anywhere in the whole country."

"You think Burial Jones Clay will see it like that?"

That stopped Lamarr for a minute. He actually had to think about it, scratching his neck. "I'd say it's doubtful."

"Then I spurn your advice."

"Hey now, no need to get choleric."

They rode around the block and across a few more streets until they came to a saloon that was already shaking sawdust into the road, with the moon hardly in the sky yet. Burial's place was three stories high and doing heavy business. Blaring music, squealing girls, loud singing, and the sporadic noise of brawls drifted through the sizzling night.

"Runs with only one or two other like-minded fools, you say?"

"Come to think of it, there might just be a few more than that." Lamarr looked up and read the sign above the bat-wings. *"La Fonda del Reyes."*

"It means 'the Inn of Kings.'"

"Ole Burial thinks a bit too much of hisself, don't he? Pretty snooty name for a whorehouse barroom."

"You sound as if you might be familiar with the place."

11

"Well, yeah," Lamarr admitted, "I may have stepped inside once or twice, for a glass of sarsaparilla."

The wind had shifted and the fiery breeze brought on the stink of a nearby corpse. Somebody had been killed in the past few hours and the body was still around, rotting in the heat.

Priest's stomach churned wildly. He had to bite his tongue in an effort to help clear his mind, which suddenly thrashed with ugly memories of the death of his parents. He was oblivious to the world but he'd seen a fair number of bodies. A part of him, damn it all, actually enjoyed the smell.

Lamarr sniffed and said, "Somebody's mama's gonna have an empty plate set tonight. Good thing you got more boxes."

"So long as we don't wind up in them."

"Nah, don't fret none. We got the angels of heaven standing right behind us."

"My heart isn't quite comforted," Priest said. "Shouldn't they be out front?"

They walked inside the Inn of Kings and Priest immediately felt ashamed and nauseous. The action, the foul odor of the room, and the mobbing bodies all reminded him of when he was a drunkard a while back. While it was true that he'd preferred wandering naked through pigsties with a bottle in each hand, maybe dancing on rooftops daring strangers to shoot him, he'd also spent enough of his time crawling across the floors of detestable places exactly like this.

The forty-foot bar was packed with drinkers, and the people kept moving up and down the wide staircase in a constant procession. The gaming tables were crammed with well-dressed, well-heeled gamblers crowding miners and rannies just in off the range. The saloon was actually much cleaner than Priest had expected. The whole place sort of shocked him. He was surprised by how many more white folks were in here. Not just drunks and thieves either, but some of the more respected citizens. There were also a hell of a lot of guns.

Priest scanned the room and located at least four main players right off. The bartender; a weasel-faced Irishman doing a bad job of covering the back door; and two angry-eyed Negroes who sat up front, not talking or sipping their beers, just smoking cigars and keeping a watch on things. They spotted Priest and Lamarr and perked up in their seats a bit.

Lamarr had no interest in poker, roulette, billiards, or any other game that cities like Tombstone and San Francisco thrived on—nothing except for faro. Something about it fascinated him, and a divine expression of purity would fill his face as he gave up all his cash trying to buck the tiger. Even now it was getting to him, the thought of running those cards. Priest saw it in his eyes.

"Hey—," Lamarr said.

"No, we don't have any money."

"You got a wallet nearly bursting out your back pocket."

"You still owe me from your trip to Sonora." He paused. "And your trip to San Francisco, and Dallas, and, in case you've forgotten, Tombstone, and—"

"Now it ain't no fair you bringing up Tombstone again. I been telling you I'll get that there money back from Fatima the next time I'm at the Bird Cage. She just holdin' it for a little while for me."

"And I know where."

Lamarr pointed out Burial Jones Clay, who was seated at a table playing poker with five other men. He was young, much too young to be Miz Utopia's true son. This was her grandson, possibly even her great-grandson. Burial Jones Clay couldn't have topped twenty-five yet. He wore a black high-crowned Stetson, a fancy black-and-white calfskin vest, and large-rowled silver-plated spurs.

14

"Some jaspers dress for poker like they goin' on a cattle drive," Lamarr said.

"If he wears spurs that size in here it means he likes using those rowels on a man when he's down."

"Yep. There's a half dozen of Burial's by-gone friends wandering town with only one eye left, maybe half a nose."

"Looks like the big trouble is sitting up front."

Lamarr nodded. "Shorter one is Rolle. Other is Jester. They never done a lick of good in this world. Don't worry about them none though. Burial keeps 'em too near the door to be much good. They only really there to look mean."

"They must get paid a lot to do it so well."

The place had already quieted down, with folks angling in their seats to watch Lamarr. He had a presence nobody in the same room could ever avoid. "That's more like it. I gonna go have a chat now."

"Got anything in mind to say?"

"A whole lot. I just gonna be my irre-sistible, naturally charming self."

"You might want to avoid that."

Lamarr burst out laughing as he moved from the bar, letting the laugh roll on too loudly for a bit too long, until it got ugly and even more heads spun his way. He

15

stood at Burial's table watching him and his men play. Without a word of introduction he sat and elbowed himself some room. Lamarr eased out the big smile again and Burial Jones Clay did the same. It was damn near almost as wide and bright.

That was quick, Priest thought. They were already into it.

Lamarr cleared his throat, redoubled his efforts, and put everything he had into his smile. It glowed so white Priest had to squint to look at it. The red sash Lamarr wore around his waist all the time was dirty and faded, and he had his two converted Navy .36s tucked in the small of his back.

Priest figured it would take them at least ten minutes before they got past each other's veneer and Lamarr finally annoyed the kid enough to start anything serious. Burial would say, "So, you want trouble?" and Lamarr would show a little sadness in his eyes and respond with something like, "I ain't ever looked for trouble but it always do manage to find me."

Priest had nothing to do but wait for it, so he decided to get a drink.

The musicians started thrashing into another tune, a couple of the dancing girls changing over. He looked back at Rolle and

Jester and noticed they were keeping their eyes on him. That was all right. The bartender was, too. Priest glanced toward the end of the bar and saw the stock of a ten-gauge shotgun angling out from beneath. The guy might be a player but he hadn't had much cause to shoot anybody in here so far. Otherwise he'd know to keep the weapon closer to the middle of the bar, where he could reach it from either end. Better yet, keep two or three weapons back there.

"Howdy!" Priest said.

Sometimes you couldn't be friendly enough. The bartender appraised him with open bitterness. Priest ordered a beer and brought it to his lips but didn't quite take a sip. He thought he might be able to handle a drink nowadays, but even the foam reminded him of the years he'd lost, his old sorrows and his recent ones, and he started getting thirsty again.

The bartender frowned and gnashed his back teeth, slanting his jaw. He had a tremendous belly that strained against his leather apron, making it creak and groan. His bald black crown swam with huge beads of sweat, each drop catching the lamplight and flashing it back against the polished top of the bar.

Priest put the beer back down, untouched. He checked the gunnies again and they were still watching him.

He told the bartender, "Sam, give me a bottle of whiskey."

"My name ain't Sam, it's Harlan." Harlan gave him a bottle of nearly clear liquid. Priest pulled the cork and sniffed. It was cheap and watered down.

"Not this. Give me rum."

"You got enough money for that?" Harlan asked.

Priest put Miz Utopia's silver dollar on the bar. Harlan brought back the better liquor, looking a little more upset. That was good. Priest uncorked it and got a whiff of the stuff. It wasn't rum but it wasn't as cut down either. He asked, "How about some good mash? You got any shine back there?"

Harlan's back teeth made a staccato clicking noise and he began to jitter a bit, his fat belly rolling all over. His breathing grew harsher and louder. He wanted to be sure he gave Priest the full display of his annoyance, which was sort of fun to behold. Harlan took the bottle back without comment, reached under the bar, came up with the moonshine, and kept the dollar. "You want anything else? I got other customers."

Priest didn't have to check the liquor this time. The cork had almost completely disintegrated and the stink of the corn mash flooded his nose and throat. "I think that'll be it."

He brought the bottle over to the gunnies' table and put it between them. "On me, men," he said, and turned to go.

Rolle said, "A moment, please." He puffed on the cigar and carefully blew the smoke down low and away so it wouldn't offend Priest.

Some of the worst men around were the most polite, but it was still a nice change. Rolle's gaze of intense curiosity and distaste never let up. Priest made him itchy. Priest made a lot of people itchy, and he wasn't exactly sure why.

"I'm Rolle," Rolle said. "And this is Jester." Jester nodded. He was the silent one who killed because he didn't like people and didn't consider them to be any different than sheep, cattle, or cans lined up on a corral fence. Still, Jester tipped his hat.

"You and your partner should leave now," Rolle continued, "before we cart your dead bodies out of here."

Okay, so he wasn't so polite anymore. "Thanks for the warning," Priest told him, and he almost meant it.

19

"We don't drink, and we don't want a drink from you."

"I didn't think you did," Priest said, and left them. It was time to join Lamarr. He was probably pissing Burial Jones Clay off pretty good by now.

Chapter Two

"That old woman had no right to ask you to brace me," Burial said, folding to a pair of eights.

"She didn't ask exactly," Lamarr told him. "I sorta volunteered, you might say."

Burial let out a bark of laughter that had more coyote than man to it. "Well now, that was a damn stupid thing to do."

Lamarr hung his head, as if in shame. "I've been known to take a misstep or two along my rocky path, it's true."

Priest grabbed an empty chair and forced himself into the ring of men around the table. The game bothered him. He'd thought Burial was a real gambler willing to take a major chance, but now Priest realized Burial was too cautious to be a risk taker, dropping to a pair of eights. If he was that wary, this was going to be more difficult than they'd thought.

He smiled pleasantly at the card players staring at him. He nodded to each. "Hi. How you? Hey there. Howdy. You doing okay?"

Burial chuckled for a while, shaking his head, sort of having a good time with all this sociability before turning to Priest. "You come here to distress me and you're not even wearing a gun?"

"This looks like a friendly place. What would I need a gun for?"

"You never do know."

"I suppose I could always borrow one."

"You're as crazy as your granpappy," Burial said. His heavy spurs jangled as he leaned forward in his chair. "I know you, Priest McClaren. I heard about you and your whole cracked family."

"That right?"

"These here are all my people. This is my place, top to bottom. Who's gonna give you a pistol?"

Priest's hands flashed out under the table, reaching for the gun belt of the man to the left of him and that of the other jasper to the right. He came up holding a .44 Colt Frontier and some tiny foreign piece he'd never seen before, pointing both barrels at Burial.

"You've got right neighborly friends, I'd

say. They all appear to be the giving kind, far as I see."

"Praise baby Jesus," Lamarr said. "They Christian folk."

Maybe all it had taken was the one breath of moonshine, but Priest suddenly felt himself loosening up, that fine rush surging through him. Maybe he liked it too much and didn't want it to end so quickly. He upended the guns and placed them on the table before the two men he'd taken them from.

Both jaspers picked up the pistols and held them pointed a few inches from Priest's head. He didn't really mind much. He still had his knife.

"You want woe and misfortune with me?" Burial asked.

Priest drew a deep breath as Lamarr answered, "Hey, that's pretty good there, I like that plenty. 'Woe and misfortune.' No, I ain't ever wanted trouble, but it always do manage to find me."

"You cotton to calamity anyway."

Lamarr's jaw muscles tightened. He'd been born and grown on a Georgia plantation owned by a man called Thompson, his mother only fifteen years older than him. Lamarr worked the fields until he was seventeen and finally strangled Thompson, and he took his time doing it, first choking the plantation master with his left fist and then his right, making it last a good long while. Nowadays, just hearing the word "cotton" made him want to kill somebody.

Burial was still having fun. He tilted his head at Priest, trying to do something with style, his hand cupping his chin. Possibly it worked with the ladies. "It's got to be embarrassin' to have that sickness runnin' through your family blood. You dance naked with Chicorah and his people yet?"

"No."

"Your granpappy got hisself a little squaw up there on White Mountain?"

"No."

"Or is he jest sittin' in them rocks planning raids on the town? You really should take that old mossy-horned codger out in the desert and shoot him."

"That what you got planned for Miz Utopia?"

Burial stiffened and finally dropped the smile.

This could be it. Priest already had the knife in his hand pressed close to his leg, and he didn't worry about anybody at the table. Or the drunk Irishman who stood too far off to be of any good to Burial. That left Harlan the bartender and Rolle and Jester at the front of the room, but he was still prepared to make his move as need be.

But Burial let the prod pass, which surprised both Priest and Lamarr. Either he wasn't as eager for serious grief as he'd acted or something else was going on. Lamarr started glancing around, trying to figure it out.

It took only a few seconds before they noticed there was some extra activity going on upstairs. Burial dealt another hand and folded to a possible flush.

A crying teenage Negro girl slid out of one of the upstairs rooms and stood at the top of the stairway making plaintive, bird-like sounds. Her cries were almost lost in the din of the saloon, but Lamarr and Priest kept their eyes on her. She took a few hesitant steps down the stairs and the Irishman grinned and blocked her way. She backed up, fluttering her wrists uselessly, before wheeling and making a dash for it. There was some distant shouting, the Irishman cackling until he went into a coughing fit.

Lamarr kept a good rein on himself. "Looks like that little girl there wants to go home."

"Who?" Burial asked.

"That poor thing with tears in her eyes. She gone now. She went back upstairs. That where you keep 'em all?"

"Oh, that's jest Daisy. She got here with

her sisters a few days back, come in from Louisiana. She needs some adjustin' still."

"So you importin' young gals now."

"Tha's right." Burial reached into his pile of winnings and shoved about two hundred dollars towards Lamarr. "That faro dealer over there, her name is Estrelita. She sure is a pretty tiny thing, ain't she? Those small hands and those pale fingers, I swear I got no idea how she ever grew so fine at card dealing with those baby girl hands."

This was bad, Priest thought. Lamarr didn't look any different, but everybody could tell he was shaking somewhere inside. The word had been out on him for a long time—he'd do anything to buck the tiger.

Lamarr turned his head to stare at the faro dealer, brooding on the wonderfully fluid movements of Estrelita's thin fingers, the cards gliding along the tabletop in rapid, controlled motions. Burial went for his pistol, a .41 Colt Lightning, about to bring it up to the back of Lamarr's head.

Priest had begun moving the moment Lamarr glanced over at the faro table. He didn't need to do much but he had to do it quickly, trying not to worry about the two gunnies near the front door, the Irishman, Harlan the bartender.

He reached down and grabbed hold of a chair leg on either side of him, upending the two jaspers whose guns he'd taken before. The Colt Lightning was clearing leather. Burial hadn't oiled his holster in a while and the barrel made a soft scratching hiss as it slid free.

Enough time if he gave it his all. Priest spun and hurled the knife, winging it sidearm almost absently, so that the blade sort of glided straight on. The butt of the knife struck the bartender—who was bringing up the double-barrel ten-gauge—in the mouth and knocked him backward into the liquor shelves. A gush of blood and tooth chips exploded from his face and he disappeared in a swell of shattering glass.

Now Priest had no knife, and a freezing sweat broke out along his upper lip and across his shoulders. He felt a buzz in his left ear and then another in his right. Burial was cocking the Colt Lightning, his smile completely gone as Priest lunged forward over the card table.

Lamarr was still entranced by Estrelita's graceful hands, the way she flipped the cards as if drawing them from the air and passed clean money back and forth. Burial was fast and strong, and he managed to twist out of Priest's way even while bring-

27

ing his pistol around to slam it against Priest's forehead. The blow stunned him as he rolled backward off the table and hit the floor.

A burning splash of desert brilliance flared behind Priest's eyes. At least his head was hard enough that Burial had lost his grip on the gun and dropped it. Priest was aware enough to protect his face, knowing Burial was going to use the rowels on him now.

He tried to block as Burial kicked out, slashing the spurs against Priest's forearms. Priest covered his eyes. Blood spattered against his lips as he tightened up, grunting in pain. The rowels hooked closer and the agony flared up his arms. The slashes were pretty deep already and getting worse. He shouldn't have thrown the knife.

Lamarr had finally come out of it, pulling his Navy .36s from his sash and firing at Rolle and Jester, who were on their feet. Only then did Priest realize that they'd been shooting at him the whole time. No wonder his ears were buzzing. The commotion grew even wilder on the second floor with women screaming and folks running all over, up and down the stairway, out the doors into the street. Gunfire continued from all around. Priest grabbed for Burial's ankles, knowing he was taking a bad chance. If he missed, those spurs would chew off half his face.

Filled with glee, doing sort of a two-step stomp now, Burial shouted, "You gonna wish you was daid!"

"One of us will."

Priest clutched Burial's left boot and undid the spur so fast that Burial was still trying to stab him with it even after it was gone. The spur chimed and rang softly. Priest reached up and jabbed the rowel into Burial's thigh. It didn't hurt him much but Burial spun awkwardly, arms flapping, and Priest was able to kick his feet out from under him. Once they were both on the floor, Priest aimed well and dove forward. He scratched Burial directly between the eyebrows with the spur and blood ran heavily into Burial's eyes, blinding him.

Lamarr was having a marvelous time, guffawing loudly from behind an overturned table and punching any man in the jaw who got too close. They were stacked two deep around him and Lamarr was still firing at the gunnies. He'd already put the Irishman down with a bullet in the right leg, and he'd pummeled a weeping heap of card players scrambling for cover. Lamarr had taken at least one bullet in his left arm but he hadn't dropped his pistols. Estrelita appeared to be very impressed by all this, and Lamarr kept winking at her.

Things weren't all that grave, considering. Priest snatched the Colt Lightning from under Burial and hurled the pistol as hard as he could at Rolle and Jester's table. He didn't know how to shoot. Like Lamarr, they hadn't really dived for cover, but were just standing there at their table carefully aiming and blasting, still smoking their cigars and calmly returning lead from way across the room.

The gun struck the bottle he'd placed on the table and sent the shine splashing all over in thick spatters. Jester was already collapsing with his shirt on fire. Lamarr had put two shots into his chest. The dying gunny's shirt blazed much brighter when the spray hit him and Rolle's cigar flared as his face was suddenly engulfed in a dazzling ball of orange flame. He howled in anguish and whirled madly around the room until Lamarr took a nice slow bead and shot him in the neck.

"Well," Priest said.

Lamarr looked over. "Damn, you actually plan that?"

"I didn't think it would work."

"It shouldn't have, except we got baby

Jesus on our side. The Lord surely do love a senseless man!"

Priest didn't want to think about that. He looked around and didn't see Burial Jones Clay anywhere on the floor. He ducked behind the bar and retrieved his knife.

Harlan the bartender was just lumbering to his feet about then, using the shotgun as a staff to prop himself up while he spit blood. Priest kicked the ten-gauge out from under him and Harlan dropped back into more shelving. He was covered in booze.

Remembering what it was like, Priest could almost feel the icy liquor drying on his chest, in his hair, the screeching nightmares flooding his throat. He took the shotgun with him and said, "Harlan, go out the back door now. You try the front and you'll be bacon by the time you hit the bat-wings."

The fire continued to spread fast, streaming and lunging as it roared and glided along. Most everybody had already gotten out of the place, except for a few of the rowdies whom Lamarr had clubbed. And the Irishman, too, who was dragging himself around the floor in agonized circles.

Estrelita and Lamarr were talking over by the faro table, casual as can be. Priest could imagine Lamarr taking the time out to play a few hands while the flames swarmed into the rafters, and hoped Lamarr could fight the tiger long enough to get the hell out of the building.

He ran upstairs and pressed his way through a few of the straggler prostitutes and cowpunchers who were struggling to get their clothes on. Smoke bloomed up around his heels. He hit the third floor and tried doors until he came to a locked one. Priest threw himself against it twice until the lock sprang.

Inside he found five young girls who clearly didn't belong anywhere near the Inn of Kings, arms around each other as they huddled together near the far wall. They were terrified of him, but he moved to the one Burial had called Daisy and said, "Come on. We're leaving this place. There's a woman named Miz Utopia who's going to take care of you until we can get you back to Louisiana."

"Tuvi," Daisy said.

"What's that?"

She pointed at the window. "Tuvi wouldn't do what the man ask. She bit and clawed him, he carry her over and threaten to drop her, and she fight some more and done jumped."

Priest pulled the drapes aside and looked out the window. He saw Tuvi's body behind the saloon in the alley three floors below, neck and arms twisted in unnatural ways. Burial hadn't even cared enough to hide the corpse.

"You're all going to be fine now, girls."

They didn't believe him as they sobbed and started coughing. Priest hoped he wasn't lying. He took Daisy's hand and the others followed as the air grew worse. He led the way through the corridor filled with clouds of thickening smoke. The heat was getting bad as the sweat slithered over him even as he felt his exposed skin dry out and begin to scorch. He ushered the girls out and waved them on down the stairway, urging and forcing them into the haze. He was about to follow when Burial suddenly appeared from out of the flames.

Burial tried an Apache war shriek as he leaped at Priest, holding the rowel before him like a knife. It didn't make all that much of an impression and wasn't all that similar to a real Apache scream. Gramps could do a whole hell of a lot better.

Priest watched Burial in midair, veering as the smoke whirled, that bloody face coming closer like a death mask, with the spur catching the brazen yellow light of the fire as Burial descended. It was sort of graceful, the bizarre dance he did, coming in for the kill.

33

But he was too slow. Priest thought about using the shotgun but decided against it. Instead he brought up the knife in a blur of black motion and turned aside the rowel. Burial's war cry became a confused gasp as he went tumbling past and hit the banister with his full weight.

The wood cracked as loudly as thunder and Burial glanced down wide-eyed at all three flights opening into empty space and flame below him. He waved his arms trying to keep his balance. The railing splintered further as Burial reached backward for Priest, trying to grab hold, groping wildly.

Priest shoved him a little and listened to the wood break sharply. Now Burial's scream was a lot closer to that of a real Apache. Even Chicorah would've been damn proud.

Priest said, "Good, that's better. You're getting it."

Just as the banister gave way and Burial began to fall, Priest grabbed him by the black-and-white calfskin vest, swung him all the way around, and brought the stock of the shotgun up into his chin. Burial Jones Clay dropped to the carpet in a heap and Priest took him by the ankle and dragged him down the stairs.

Lamarr was still at the faro table and Estrelita was trembling and sobbing as she stood, and dealt the cards, too afraid to leave. The ends of her hair were singed and trailing wisps of white smoke. She had a wet cloth draped over her face but her eyebrows were already heavy with ash. Lamarr lost another hand. She took his money while the fire licked and clawed all around them, ravenously gnawing at the ceiling. Whatever chance Lamarr might've had with her was long gone by now.

Daisy and the others hung at the end of the bar, too terrified to dodge the flames. Priest motioned for the girls to go out the back door while he hauled Burial across the ruins of his saloon, but they merely stared at him without comprehension. He shoved Daisy, and the girls vanished after her into the alley.

Plate glass shattered in all corners of the room and the walls were tearing through. Smoke bloomed madly and lunged and stretched everywhere. The roof groaned and cried out, about to come down. Lamarr lost another hand. Estrelita met Priest's eyes and silently begged him to let her run before they all burned to death. Sometimes it got like this.

With his chest beginning to tighten, Priest took the cards from her and tossed them into the blazing piles that had once been the bodies of Rolle and Jester.

Relief flooded Lamarr's face as the spell broke and he'd finally been stopped. He'd been betting with the money Burial had given him and he'd forfeited it all. Estrelita grabbed the cash and fled into the dense haze.

"You ready to go?" Priest asked, coughing so hard he could barely understand his own words.

"I suppose it's time."

Lamarr picked up Burial and lugged him over his shoulder. He led the way out of the place as the smoke and flame raged around them, twining, reaching, perhaps even loving. Priest started to stagger some and he felt the steady arm of Lamarr encircle him and pull him out of the Inn of Kings.

A couple of hundred people milled around in the street. Some had been inside, and more had come just to see the building become ashes. A few men stood with their jaws dropped, their features contorted with awful sorrow.

Nobody rushed to get a bucket of water. The Irishman wept and made baby noises. Harlan tried to comfort him but couldn't say much on account of his busted teeth. A preacher led his choir in a chorus of "Bringing in the Sheaves."

Miz Utopia Jones Clay stood with the

rest of them, her arms around the five huddled girls, who were weeping and telling her their ugly stories. They wanted their mothers and fathers. They wanted to go back home. Somebody had to bury Tuvi.

Miz Utopia hugged the teenagers tightly, a small smile on her battered face as she stared at the unconscious form of her grandson lying near her feet. Priest and Lamarr sat heavily in the dirt, clothes and hair still smoking. Miz Utopia whispered to Daisy, pointed while giving directions, and sent her up the block. The girl returned a few minutes later carrying Miz Utopia's remedy pouches.

It took the old woman only five minutes to tend to Priest's and Lamarr's wounds. She'd soaked her bandages in some kind of medicinal brew that stank and burned, but Priest immediately felt better.

"Miz Utopia," Lamarr said, "I don't think you'll be needin' that coffin anytime soon."

"I paid for it, and I think we needs it right now."

"But—well, ma'am, you ain't daid, and these girls here, they need someone till we can get 'em home again."

She frowned at him. "Lamarr Russell, you dang fool, you don't think that there coffin was meant for me none, now do you?"

Priest figured it out then. He climbed up the buckboard and got his hammer and nails ready.

Lamarr cocked his head and went, "Heh." He picked up Burial and dropped him on the back of the rig, reloaded his Navy .36s, climbed aboard and put two shots into the coffin lid. He tossed Burial in the box just as he started to come around.

"What's this?" Burial whined as the hysteria took over his voice. "Oh Lord, what's this?" he shouted as Priest hammered the nails in. "I ain't daid yet! I ain't daid! Where you takin' me?"

"Boot Hill," Lamarr said.

"The hell!"

"It's in Virginia City, Montana."

"Dodge City," Priest told him. "Kansas."

"Don't you worry none, we find it!"

The choir had worked themselves into "Down by the River." One of the church singers was tone deaf and kept striking a hollow note that moved the crowd along. Priest grabbed the reins and drove the buckboard on, noticing that Lamarr still looked a little put out.

Maybe they'd just ride around town for a

while, or maybe they'd head out into the desert. Priest didn't know exactly how this would play out, listening to the muted cries of Burial Jones Clay lying in his comfortable coffin.

"Maybe we'll go to Tombstone first," Priest said. "I've never been there."

"Oh, you'll like it at the Bird Cage. And I'll get to see my sweet Fatima again."

"And get my money back."

"Now how many times I tole you, she just holdin' on to it for me. You sure are a mistrustful soul."

"Born that way, I guess."

They rode until the harsh light of the burning Inn of Kings had long faded behind them. Lamarr turned to him and said, "You let me know how far you wanna go with this."

Priest really hadn't been around much. He'd never stepped foot out of Patience his entire life and thought that maybe it was about time. Tombstone sounded all right, but he had an aching to see the plains of Kansas. He recalled Miz Utopia's beaten face again. He thought of Daisy at the top of the stairs weeping, the crumpled body of Tuvi lying in a dirty alley, and all the innocent men waiting at the bottom of Boot Hill.

Tom Piccirilli

"We've got a long while to go yet," Priest said, knowing it was true no matter which direction they went in.

He snapped the reins harder.

Chapter Three

They rode south, camped out on the desert that night, and in the morning headed for Padre Villejo's mission, where there was a funeral being held. They parked the rig close enough for Burial to hear the shovelfuls of earth being turned and thrown.

"Oh Lord above, you can't put a living man in the ground," Burial whimpered. "I ain't daid. . . ."

"Think we ought to shoot him first?" Lamarr asked.

"Sure sounds like he doesn't want to go in the ground still breathing."

"We can fix that easy."

They got down off the buckboard and walked to the church. Priest didn't know if they just had bad timing or what, but the last visit they'd paid Padre Villejo had been during a funeral, too.

"Mama used to believe in signs like this," Lamarr said.

"Like what?"

"How we always walking in on the dead."

Priest didn't want to consider that for too long. "I don't suppose she thought it was a particularly good omen."

"Good enough, I reckon. At least we ain't the ones in the box."

The stone and mud of the adobe church proved that faith and mourning lived on in the very walls of some structures. You could feel the great weight of contrition, belief, and the past draped on your shoulders, laid across your back. It never failed to unsettle Priest. They moved into the doorway, removed their hats, and hung in the shadows, watching.

Padre Villejo's voice rose soft as a subdued prayer, so soothing that a few of the children and old men began to nod off in their seats. The pews were filled with peasant farmers and their families, elderly women in black shawls, all of them Mexican. Padre Villejo stood in the pulpit sagging to one side on his crutches. He looked around, took in the congregation, and smiled at members here and there.

He stood six feet tall on his one leg. The

other had been cut off when he was a child, after his father had complained about the village taxes. His closely trimmed mustache and goatee were fiercely brown, his skin nearly as dark as Lamarr's. The large rosary beads tied around his waist ended in a heavy wooden cross that swung wildly when he gestured.

Two nuns, Sister Teresa and Sister Lorraina, always sat on either side of him, keeping vigil. They were there to make certain he didn't get into such an aggravated state that he knocked himself over the way he used to do all the time. Today, though, he was so restrained that both women were drooped in their chairs with their eyes half-closed.

Priest knew Father Villejo wasn't so much a man of God as he was a political rebel bent on helping folks in whatever fashion he could. He went up against generals, guerrillas, bandits, revolutionaries, government officials, and anybody else causing trouble in the hills or getting rich off his people.

Sometimes the harassment hit closer to home and things got downright uncivilized. Priest had once seen him use those crutches to puncture the liver of a youth who had stolen a few pennies from the poor box. The kid had also used a bullwhip to send wine and wafer all over the place, and that's really what did it. The youth, like so many around that age, was trying out the new calling of "bandito," flexing muscle and slapping around the elderly and weak.

The padre stomped the thief first with one crutch and then the other, skillfully jabbing him in the soft spots of the belly, the kidneys, and the groin. It took ten minutes for Sister Teresa and Sister Lorraina to pull the padre off the boy, who was vomiting by then. The kid held the whip out in both hands like an offering, spewing blood.

But none of the old hellfire was in him this morning. He appeared almost sluggish, defeated, on the verge of tossing aside his worn Bible.

Sister Lorraina tried to start a hymn but she faltered and the few who joined in gave up quickly. Padre Villejo slumped over the poorly crafted lectern and the wood started to split beneath him. One crutch fell and Sister Teresa retrieved it, carefully set it under his arm again. He smiled thankfully, wearily, and brought his service to a close. The tension and misery had grown ponderous enough to crush the people in their seats. No one moved for a time, and then slowly they began to stir. The padre nodded and two barrel-chested men rose from the middle pews, progressed to the front, and hefted the coffin.

"Whoever it was sure didn't weigh much," Lamarr said.

"Christ, I hope it wasn't a child."

"Not enough cryin' for that. But whatever it is, it's gotta be bad."

The two men carted the coffin out the side entrance, followed by the silent mourners.

Priest walked to the front of the church. Padre Villejo glanced up. "*Preste.* I never see you for mass but you always appear for all the processions. I must bury a friend today."

It sort of bothered Priest that he'd known this man for ten years and had never once had supper or a drink with him. Their relationship seemed as fixed and unyielding as the stone foundation of the building itself. There was something wrong with that, and he resolved to change it if he could, but quick as the notion came upon him he realized it would never happen.

Lamarr stepped up beside him and that massive presence filled the small room. Sister Teresa hovered nearby and let out a long streaming whisper of Spanish like a draft sweeping past. Padre Villejo barely let his gaze brush Lamarr. "You have both been bleeding again. You are always bleeding and dripping blood on our floors. You smell of smoke. Go with the sisters, they will tend to you."

"Not today," Lamarr said. "Miz Utopia done a good job at binding us up. Salve's already got most of the wounds closed."

"It is good to hear."

As the padre crutched himself toward the open doorway, dust blew in across the rotted floorboards. Priest stared off at the villagers, who really looked no more or less grieved than usual. They were lowering the coffin down into the ground with two frayed ropes. The box had no lid and he could now see it was an old woman in there, dressed in yellowed lacy clothes that reminded him of a dusty wedding gown. Her dead eyes were about half-open and the tip of her tongue jutted from the corner of her mouth.

"Who was she?" Lamarr asked.

"No one of consequence."

Priest drew back his chin as if slapped, lifted his head. He took that answer as an insult.

So did Lamar. "Now don't you go talking like I'm some government man come to put a tariff on your broken-down heifer, padre. If I got cause to ask, then you've got cause to answer."

"Is it so?"

"Yeah, it's so."

You could see Padre Villejo considering that, pondering whether it was true or not. "I am sorry," he said. "I sometimes forget that you two do not frown upon us like the others from the town do."

"We got no cause to frown on anybody," Lamarr told him, letting some of the smile out. "Hardly anybody, leastways."

So they were going to get into it. The father stood up straighter, a little of his usual steel back in his eye. "She was just a woman from the village. Donna Angelina Allasandro. She owned nothing and had no family. But she had honor and did not deserve to die this way."

"What way?" Priest said.

"Alone. At the hands of some bandit. The way so many of the old die here."

Priest could feel himself tightening up, inch by inch, losing patience with how the padre eked out whatever it was he was trying to say without going all the way with it. It still startled Priest to realize how little composure he really had, how temporary it was. "A bandit. Who?"

Pointing south, the wooden cross at the padre's waist flapped. "Some vaqueros from the pueblo beyond the other side of the river. Don Luis Braulio is master of that village, who rustles cattle, peddles small arms and ammunition, and steals whatever he can. He has gotten wealthy very quickly, and it's brought out the beast in him and his cadre. He is brutal and unmerciful, and likes to use a slow knife on his enemies. His is not a new tale."

"And these vaqueros?"

"They are all faceless, all the same. There are more of them every day. Some were once good men, driven by hunger to do evil. They go out and loot and swindle, and murder whoever stands up to them. This woman's son did so and was killed for his efforts. He was the last of her family and she died shortly after him."

"And the rest of your congregation?"

"They are afraid. Many of their children, those of age, have already left. For California. Some of them talk of gold as if it is given away on street corners. Others . . . well, we pray for them, and hope they return to God."

"And we already know how Sheriff Burke would handle this here situation, as it is," Lamarr said. "He ain't much on investigatin' and trying to get to the heart of the matter, especially for folks this close to the border."

Priest nodded, imagining the scene, as it flashed before him. There they were, bringing the coffin into town, explaining to Burke about Burial and the Inn of Kings, trying to get him to inquire about the murdered Tuvi, the stolen girls turned into whores, the old Mex woman, and vaqueros causing trouble way outside the county line. Out of the country, even. Burke standing there in his freshly pressed brown suit, that bow tie perfectly centered under his collar as always. The thick mustache leaning too far to the left, with Burke inclining his head to the right hoping to balance it out. The sheriff not even bothering to laugh as he walked away from the whole mess in disgust.

"Sheriff Burke don't much mind them kind of nefarious doings," Priest said, recalling Lamarr's words, which had, pretty much, started them down the trail of their latest woes.

"But we, being good and decent citizens," Lamarr said, "mind such doings greatly."

"I must go," Padre Villejo told them. "Her friends await final prayers."

They watched him head into the small graveyard with the rickety fence made of chicken wire, the sisters at his sides with the hot wind snapping their lengthy vestments. Priest listed to one side of the doorway and Lamarr leaned on the other.

"I can't quite shake the feelin' that the padre is playing us just a touch," Lamarr said. His large hands were working, tips of his fingers rubbing together as if he wanted to roll a cigarette but didn't have the fixings.

"I was sort of thinking the same thing."

"Maybe we just gullible looking."

"Maybe so."

"Got to work on that some."

"How do we go about doing that? Grow a goatee?"

"I don't know. Maybe Fatima can help."

"Uh-huh."

Someone strummed a guitar and the mourners for Donna Angelina Allasandro sang a sorrowful, languorous tune. Lamarr liked it and began to sway. His mother's slave songs were about the only thing that helped him make it off the plantation alive, and he whispered, "Praise Jesus" from time to time. When the music ended, Lamarr headed back to the buckboard, ready to finish it up with Burial.

Priest started after him but turned when he saw the flutter of a silk scarf. A woman rose from where she'd been seated alone at the back of the church, black shawl wrapped around her head. He recognized the scarf drifting around her neck only because he'd bought it himself in Tucson last year.

He eased up against the whitewashed wall, his heart steadily beating harder and harder. The petite woman took small steps, her slim hips working easily beneath her dress. She walked out of the church and around the opposite corner. Priest trailed behind.

Even though she was now married to Septemus Hart—Lamarr's own hated father—Priest still couldn't help wondering if it was really over between them. Or if he could somehow win back what he'd lost long ago. He had a habit of hunting after what was already irrevocably gone. It was a flaw in his character he couldn't eradicate, not that he tried much.

"Sarah."

Her shoulders stiffened but she didn't turn to face him. She spoke softly, and though she'd never been to Dublin, her slight brogue caught hold. In common conversation you could barely notice it, unless she was angry. "Priest McClaren, are ye followin' me now?"

Her voice, as always, swept him along,

51

back to the days when they made love in the shadow of the saguaro. She'd move her hand through his hair, stroking his temples, and say, "My man, my beautiful man, close your eyes. After all that loving work, you've earned yourself some rest now." He'd sleep for an hour and awaken to her squeezing plum juice into his mouth.

Priest licked his lips, feeling himself wafting away. "No, I have a different business here."

"So yer sayin'."

"Yes, so I say."

How had he missed seeing her when he'd entered the church? Had she come in after them? Why was she there at all? The hot breeze blew a momentary barrier of dust between them. She still wouldn't look at him. Those dark eyes full of that Irish scowl drew down on him, pervaded with a tinge of surprise and concern, but no love, no fear. She'd been crying and her cheeks were wet.

His stomach twisted so violently that he let out a grunt. He'd seen her cry only once before, the morning of the miscarriage, on the day that began their slow separation and eventual parting. The child spoke to him on occasion, during his drunken madness and even after, but said nothing now.

The curls of her black hair swept out from beneath the shawl, framing her face. She always appeared so girlish, defenseless, although he knew she was much stronger and more capable in some ways than he'd ever be.

"You're hurt," she said. Her deft fingers plucked at the dried bloodstains on his clothes.

"No, it's—"

"And what troubles have you been tangling up with on this day?"

"Never mind that, Sarah, what's wrong?" He couldn't keep out the endlessly plaintive tone. "What are you doing all the way out here?"

"You've your misfortunes and I have mine."

"That may be true, but it's not an answer."

"Yet that's all I'm willing to give."

She stepped away and he couldn't help himself, he lurched forward. For a second he thought her chin was bruised, that Septemus had been laying hands on her. Priest bit down a growl, reached out, and grabbed the edges of the shawl, drawing the cloth from her before she could slip from him.

No bruises, but her face was ashen. The circles under her exhausted eyes were so

53

dark they appeared blue. He'd never seen her so drained of life before, not even during the awful weeks after the miscarriage. It scared the hell out of him. He gripped her arms and pulled her closer.

"Take yer hands off."

"No."

"Is this what you've become then? A brute?"

"Tell me," he demanded, a little startled by how resolute he sounded. It was, somehow, the voice of his father.

"I've nothing to say to you," Sarah hissed, and the tears bloomed from her eyes and ran freely over her cheeks again.

Priest was still in love with her—he'd always be in love with her—and the force of his own emotions nearly toppled him sideways. He took her roughly by the arm and she glared at him. "Tell me, damn it."

"Let me be."

"No."

"*Please.*" The word burst from her with such fierce pleading that he could only stare in disbelief.

It was how he himself had once sounded, seeking her across town, crawling in the street drunk out of his head, and knowing he'd lost her forever. Beneath her voice their child was beginning to whisper to him again, urging Priest not to give up now, because too much depended on it.

"No," he said.

At last she relented and softened against his chest. She didn't exactly hug him. There was no passion in the clench, but she weakened and finally gave something over. It mattered as much as anything in his life ever had before, ethereal as the sensation might be. He knew this was as close as he'd ever get to having her again.

"Come to the homestead a week from to-morrow," she told him.

The last time Priest had been out to Septemus's estate, he'd killed three men, including the desperado who'd murdered Priest's parents. "What?"

"*Please.* One week from tomorrow."

"But what about Septemus?"

She broke his hold and swept off behind the church, heading for one of the small outbuildings. He noticed then that a two-horse carriage lay waiting out in back of a stand of scrub, as if intentionally hidden. The horses shifted moodily, rubbing at the wall. Two of Septemus's men helped Sarah in and climbed on board, then swung back onto the road toward Patience.

It took Priest a minute to settle himself

down enough to walk without a throbbing pain in his guts. He wandered back to the buckboard.

Lamarr must've seen Sarah but said nothing. Priest tried to explain but silence clogged his throat. He really didn't have anything to tell and wouldn't until a week from tomorrow.

He looked at the coffin in back. "You think we should let him out yet?"

"How long's it been?"

"Almost a full day."

"That all?"

"Yep."

"Think he's learned a lesson?"

Priest put his ear to the smooth pine and heard sniffling. The stink was getting worse. "It probably won't take, but he's studied on it about as much as he can, given the circumstances."

"Maybe a little later then."

They took Burial Jones Clay down to the river and Priest got out his hammer and pried the lid off. He blocked the sun with his body so Burial wouldn't go blind from the brightness. Burial moaned uncontrollably anyhow. He was awake but so cramped up he couldn't do more than tremble and lie there with his lips moving, nothing coming out. The dried blood on his face had cracked and clotted up into rusted wrinkles cut deeply by the trenches his tears had made.

Priest spent a minute rubbing circulation back into the man's arms and then got out of the way.

Lamarr reached into the coffin and pulled Burial Jones Clay out and tossed him on the ground. He kicked him once in the chin to get his attention but Burial didn't even appear to feel it.

Lamarr pointed and said, "A few miles yonder is Mexico. You'll like it there. Learn to farm. Get yourself a nice fat wife to cook you tortillas covered in honey. Enchiladas and corn bread. It's good, you'll like it. Try and come back to be a slaver once more and we'll do this all over again,'cept there won't be no airholes in the lid next time."

It didn't seem likely that Burial would try to regain any of his lost respect at the moment, considering he was covered in his own piss and shit and blood. He just nodded dumbly.

"We got an understandin', son?"

"Yass . . . yassuh."

"Well, all right then, my heart's settled."

They left him there, got back onto the buckboard, and rode on.

Priest said, "We could just be causing

trouble for a lot of innocent Mexicans, you know."

"Nah, they know how to handle the likes'a him. Cut off his eyelids and stake him out in the desert. They ain't forgivin' folk like us."

"Sure."

Priest tried to frame his thoughts and tell Lamarr something about what had occurred with Sarah, but nothing took shape. "Now what?"

"How about we go home, clean up a bit, and head over to Miss Patty's? We earned ourselves a night on the town, I say. She got a good and gracious woman name'a Lorelei workin' for her, who has touched my soul deeply."

Priest stared at him. "Did you manage to sneak off to Tombstone when I wasn't looking and get my money back from Fatima?"

"Well, no."

"Then you're expecting Miss Patty to give you credit at her house?"

"I think I just about run out my line there. Might as well go see though. Maybe she's extended it a couple dollars more."

"I tend to doubt that."

"Me, too. She's as mistrustful a soul as you are."

Chapter Four

A brimstone preacher named Deed had decided to make trouble for Miss Patty.

He'd been out in front of the parlor house for about an hour already in the late afternoon sun. Priest had been watching him the whole time, enjoying the show. Deed wore a black frock coat and flat-top Stetson, and actually did thump his Bible now and again. His voice carried to the rooftops on the burning wind, and he knew how to position himself just right so that his exhorting would echo up the street and catch the attention of passersby. His words had a slight twang and snapped hard against his teeth. Oklahoma. Maybe Kansas.

Deed's fury over such open vice worked him over like the current of a river, jouncing and flinging him down in the dust. Sometimes it was like dancing, and his bony knees nearly reached his chin. Other times he kneeled and swung an accusing finger around, pointing out faces in the crowd, laying shame and doom. Once he pointed directly at Priest, and there were some mutters and whispers from the town folk. It was nothing new.

Lamarr loved Miss Patty, and many other women of the house, too, but he couldn't help himself from joining in. Singing high unto the Lord, his mother's songs, and listening to the ministry in the fields had been the only things that had kept him and his people alive on the plantation. Even with Miss Patty scowling at him through the front window, every so often Lamarr kicked in with a "Praise Jesus!"

All that the Christian Ladies Coalition needed to fire them up was a protest against some form of wickedness in Patience. Soon twenty-five women marched with Deed in front of the whorehouse. They scurried across the street and made prune faces, reciting Scripture and peering gravely at their frightened husbands, who cowered outside the ring and toed the sand.

Lamarr looked a little dangerous jumping around like that, swinging and swaying with the red sash tied around his waist and the two Navy .36 revolvers tucked at the small of his back, but nobody appeared to mind much. His smooth, shining dark face and beaming white smile made him seem like a child. Priest unconsciously pawed at the curls of silver hair that hung in his eyes, somehow feeling a good deal older than Lamarr.

Several patrons still tried to make it inside, but no man likes to be pointed out and railed at. Miners, merchants, cowpunchers, hardheads, and harlot chasers frowned at Lamarr and the protesting ladies. Some crossed the street.

Lamarr stood abashed. "Hold on now," he called after them, "I was just giving some love up to the Lord. I didn't mean for Miss Patty to lose any business."

Priest said, "Looks like a lot of fellas are going to have to give up their love tonight, too."

"Now that just makes me feel bad."

"Bet it makes them feel a lot worse."

"Can't see any help for it now."

Priest couldn't see much either. "If you had any intention of spending a few late-night hours with that Lorelei you mentioned, I'd say you can forget it."

61

"Well, that just ain't fair! I done took me a bath today."

"Damn waste of water."

"At least I didn't go and squander any soap, too." Pawing his chin, Lamarr came up with an idea that brightened his face. "You go on in there and get Miss Patty to simmer down some."

"Hell, no!"

"Just remember, she leads with her left. Keep your hands up."

"She always gets in under my guard."

"She's got good footwork, too. And watch out she don't kick you in your personables."

Shadows crept forward as evening came on. Patty glanced out the window again and Priest caught her eyes. Her draping black hair encircled and outlined her features in a way that made him think of the lost mornings when she'd turn over in his arms and smile up at him just after dawn in back of the livery.

The memory caused a pang, but you can give your life over to only one overwhelming woe at a time. When he came back to himself he realized she was actually fogging the pane, panting, worried. She played with one curl, twisting it through her fingers. He hadn't see her like this since they were kids.

There was a new buzzing up at the corner. Heads turned and folks drifted away. Deed moved toward it angrily as if he wanted to fight whatever was stealing his audience. Priest stepped toward the latest commotion, knowing what it was, what it *had* to be. He'd been expecting Gramps for almost a week now.

Somebody laughed and others stared at Priest as he shouldered his way through the throng. That was all right. Many thought he was cracked; the rest were afraid. Most of the time it worked out.

Gramps was back from White Mountain. He'd been up there with Chicorah's people for a couple of months now, one of his longest periods ever. But he could handle it for only so long, pretending to be somebody else, and then the rest of his whole white life pushed back through.

Gramps had started to go white again but he hadn't gotten all the Apache out of himself yet. He still wore his breechcloth, and he lay curled under the trough. Deed knelt beside him and placed his palms on Gramps's forehead, trying to get Jesus in or the *Ga'ns* mountain spirits out. Gramps moaned in Apache and occasionally groaned Grandmother's name: "Ethel, Ethel." But after about twenty minutes or so, Deed got tired of laying his hands on Gramps, and Priest couldn't blame him for that.

Another hymn began and he heard Lamarr's bass kick in. Priest lifted Gramps into his arms and carried him back down the block and up Miss Patty's steps.

Deed had followed. He reached out and grabbed Priest's shoulder firmly, digging in with hard and cracked yellow nails. "Brother, your soul is in jeopardy."

So, it was going to be like that. "Thanks for the warning."

"If you want the old man's demons cast out you need to bring him into a church, not a house of ill repute."

"They're not demons."

"What?"

"According to Chicorah, the son of Apache sub-chief Sondeyka, my grandfather is a holy man blessed with *Ga'ns* mountain spirits."

"And you?"

"Yes, me, too."

"No, I meant do you actually believe what a heathen savage might say about your immortal soul?"

"Sure," Priest said.

Deed's gaze had taken on a flinty, inflexible edge, with the hint of a smile lacing his lips. A ripple passed over his face and

Priest got a glimpse beyond the sermonizing act. He didn't like what he saw in there.

For the first time Priest considered the preacher closely. Deed had large, cloudy eyes with a trace of fire and lightning in them. His fingers were long and the color of bone, and he still hadn't let go of Priest's shoulder. Tufts of white-blond hair stuck out from beneath the hat at ugly angles.

Shadows continued to twine among the porch railings and across the men's legs. Lamarr and the ladies were halfway through "My Heart to Thee, My Shepherd." Lamarr was good at harmonizing and hit the low notes really well. The ripple stirred along Deed's face again and brought on an appearance of concern. His eyes had already reverted to the grim ardor of a fanatic.

"Well, well," Priest said. "So, what's your game?"

"Now, brother, the righteous path is difficult to find, and even more arduous to walk, but the path can be shown to you. Let me guide you—"

"No use back-stepping at this point."

The hint of that mischievous grin came back. "I suppose not." Apparently, Deed didn't much mind being seen through, and that worried Priest. He searched for that flame in Deed's eyes but it was gone now as well. He wanted to know what it meant. Priest knew it was going to get somebody hurt and he tried not to sigh.

Gramps gave a snort in his sleep and finally Priest remembered he was still holding the old man. Deed clucked his tongue and said, "Tell Patty that Cousin Josiah says hello."

"Sure."

"And I'll be around to pay a call on her soon."

"I see."

The smarmy expression came out then, oozing like oil, and Deed tilted back his head, squinting. "I know about you and her, from way back. I suggest you keep out of this one affair."

"Thanks for that warning, too."

"Call it what you like," Deed said. "Just so you listen."

"Uh-huh."

"Or suffer the outcome."

"By the way," Priest told him, "have all the fun that you want out here in the street, but just so you know, if you give her any serious trouble, I'll have to put you down."

"My pards and I might take you up on that challenge."

"Call it what you like."

Priest turned to go and Deed tightened his grip, about to say something else, opening his mouth to put on a real show and call Jehovah out of the sky. Priest spun and let one of Gramps's knobby knees rap Deed in the jaw, knocking him backward down the steps with a snort.

It gave Priest some satisfaction, and his grandfather seemed to like it, too. In his sleep, Gramps smiled.

Deed's long coat had opened. He wore a long-barreled Schofield in a greased, open-end swivel holster on his left hip. Slick and sly, he liked the trick shot. Deed wiped blood from his bottom lip, buttoned his coat again, and backed off into the street where the Christian ladies fluttered around him, cooing.

Priest stood in the doorway another minute, thinking on what had just happened, before he grabbed the handle. Lamarr quickly followed him inside and said, "Baby Jesus seen what you done to that preacher, and I bet he ain't too happy 'bout it."

"Me and baby Jesus haven't been on speaking terms in years," Priest admitted, as the whores and their men wheeled past him, shrieking with laughter.

* * *

Fat Jim was playing the piano wildly, bouncing up out of his seat as usual. He weighed a hundred and five pounds and barely came up to the shoulder of most of the girls. His cigar spewed ash all over and tobacco juice ran down his stubbled chin. He looked a little touched banging at the keys like that, trying so hard to drown out Deed and the coalition outside as the night came on.

The main parlor was only now starting to clear as the folks retired upstairs for baths and a final glass of wine before the finer points of the business began. A lot of other men were just leaving, having begged off work an hour or two early and now needing to return home. Those remaining shuffled backward out of the way as Priest carried Gramps in.

Lamarr found Lorelei tending bar and he proceeded toward her, cutting off a bank manager who was explaining principle interest and dividend exclusion to anybody who might listen. The banker angled his chin when he saw the two revolvers tucked into Lamarr's sash but he kept right on talking.

Wainwright, the houseman, stood six foot five, within easy reach of three hundred pounds. He had a natural inclination to hunch forward a little, with those massive arms hanging at his sides. There was something of the animal in him, but he always remained respectful, polite, and quiet in the extreme. Priest had never heard him speak above a whisper, not even when he was breaking somebody's arm. When Wainwright sat in his enormous wrought-iron chair, he seemed as much a part of the house as the walls or the ceiling.

The houseman said, "Your old man's room is occupied at the moment. There will be clean sheets on the bed in about a half hour. You want me to ride over to Molly's and let her know Grandpa is home?"

"No thanks," Priest told him. "I'll wait until he's all the way back in his head."

His seventeen-year-old sister had enough to do with caring for her new baby. Priest put Gramps down on a divan. He expected Patty to still be holding vigil at the front window, but she wasn't there anymore. That bothered him, too. "Tell Miss Patty I need to talk to her now."

"I'm not sure she wants to see you."

That stopped him. "Say again?"

"It has something to do with the preacher. And you. She's stared down marshals, judges, ministers, angry wives and mothers-in-law without so much as turning a shade of pink. Today's about the first I've ever seen her unnerved."

69

"Go find her, and tell Fat Jim to lay off the action so we can clear the parlor."

"Your sweaty naked grandfather pretty much did that on his own." Wainwright shambled off in search of the mistress of the house.

Already this wasn't working out too well. Priest didn't completely understand why he'd given Wainwright orders or why Wainwright had taken them. A very ugly image lay just out of sight, and he felt that if he just kept moving fast enough he might avoid ever having to look at it.

Lamarr overheard Wainwright talking to Fat Jim and allowed Lorelei to usher the banker upstairs. Lamarr gazed after her as she glided up the steps, trying hard not to leer or grimace as her curves came out in full, and he failed on all counts. He glanced at Priest and said, "The trials of this world keep pilin' higher. I may need some whiskey to soothe my ravaged heart."

"And you thought you felt bad before."

"My misery deepens but I shall endure."

"You and me both."

The big room was empty and the chandeliers began to sway.

It took five minutes for Wainwright to return with Miss Patty. They both appeared angry and hurt, their faces closed. Patty also looked tired and nervous, glowering with her nostrils flared. The beautiful lines extending from the corners of her nose to the corners of her mouth were darkly incised trenches. She seemed to be sneering though she wasn't.

Priest felt as if something or perhaps someone—perhaps the teenage boy he'd been—stood just behind his left shoulder trying to get his attention. He purposefully ignored it.

"Go on home," Patty told him.

In this light, with the sun nearly gone, her hair caught the color of her blue petticoats. She backhanded a tinted curl off her forehead, showing off the cool pale angle of her neck and perfect rose *O* of her lips.

The burr in her voice scratched at him. It sounded almost like resentment, except Patty didn't have it in her to ever get jealous.

"What's the matter with you?"

"Nothing I can't handle." She poured herself a rum and didn't offer any around. Wainwright receded into the shadows at the far end of the room, sat in his iron chair, and didn't appear to be listening. Patty had another drink, sinking into a seat, and Priest understood what she was attempting to draw out of the bottle. He'd tried it for five years.

"Tell me anyway."

"Now do what I said, Priest. Go on home."

"Sure," he said. "Just answer me first."

She hadn't so much as set eyes on him yet, so Priest slid his hand out across the black-lacquer tabletop until it rested beside the shot glass. She set her lips and looked into his face. "That bastard's my cousin."

"Deed?"

"Yeah, that's what he calls himself now. Wired me for money a couple of weeks back."

"Maybe you should've given it to him."

"I did, just so he'd keep away. Now he's grudging me because I'm flush, and he wants to cut himself into my business. Claims it's the least I can do for the last living member of my family."

Priest's chest continued to tighten. He was certain she wasn't lying, but there was a lot more that wasn't being told, and he felt surprised and a little betrayed that Patty had never mentioned this cousin before.

You could know everything about a person and still not know a damn thing. When they were sixteen they'd planned on marrying. Before her miner father had been blown up at the bottom of a shaft while checking dynamite charges, and before Priest's parents had been murdered and he'd taken to the bottle. You did what you had to do in order to face each new day. You made your cash. You eventually got up out of the mud. You crawled as far as you could from beneath the shadow of gravestones.

Lamarr did his best to lessen the friction. "He'll have to do a whole lot more'a that hellfire preaching to close your doors, Patty!"

"That's what's got me worried. He's planning something. He wants to rob the ladies from the pulpit on Sundays, then take himself a kicker from my house every week." It dawned on her who she was talking to and the red anger flooded her cheeks. "And you! Don't you dare say anything to me, Lamarr Russell, you dancing turncoat Judas!"

"But, Miss Patty! I was only singin'!"

"I'll come over there and give you something to sing about!"

"Not my personables!"

Priest said, "Deed wears an open-end swivel holster. Schofield."

Lamarr smiled, letting it out inch by inch as his teeth flashed. He liked the idea of taking Deed down, now that both him and God had been transgressed. "Tricky, this voice of the Lord. Goes for the sneak shot when he's sittin' having a parley. Schofield is too long to draw quick, but easy to aim out the bottom."

"He mentioned having partners," Priest said.

Patty had rallied now. She set the rum aside and had overcome, at least for the moment, whatever it was that had been forcing her to shove Priest away. "The only ones he ever ran with were two swindlers named Lane Gruber and Foley Longstreet."

"Gruber?" Lamarr lifted his chin and nodded to himself, clucking a bit, as if he'd just gotten a long and involved joke told awhile back. "Gruber. Lane Gruber. If it's the same one, and why would there ever be two, I ask, then he was a major during the war."

"I don't know about that," Patty said, "but I suppose he'd be the right age."

"He ran under Bragg. Met some of his men in late November sixty-three, in Chattanooga. They had the heights commanding the supply lines, but in three days we drove 'em out. His tough times must've only started there if he's runnin' with a swindling preacher nowadays."

The action would keep to a minimum until midnight, when the poker players and drunks would begin to steadily stroll in again. Deed and his pards would show up sometime before then.

"He'll come tonight," Priest said. "To sniff around."

"I don't owe him a thing."

There was a tremble in her voice that resonated within him, far down where she was still a girl lying in back of the barn, where they'd made love in the dust. Priest glanced up and stared into her eyes and knew with a cold and precise knowledge that he was going to have to kill Deed.

"I believe you."

"He owes me."

He'd never heard anything like that come alive within her before, not when her mother ran off, not even when her father had been blown to pieces. Priest could feel the aching under his heart come alive with a ridiculous swiftness. The image started to catch up to him again. He was slowing down, he had to move.

From the divan, Gramps said quite distinctly, "Put your knife away."

Priest looked down to check. He wasn't holding his knife. Priest turned to say something back to the old man, but Gramps was already asleep again, breathing in bites and sweating heavily, hissing in Apache.

Chapter Five

He carried his grandfather upstairs and put him to bed in a room that Patty kept set aside for the old man. The sheets were clean. A heated breeze brushed against his throat. Priest leaned against the open window and watched the traffic in the street. There was shouting in the distance.

A full moon burned over the desert tonight. Gramps's frail bronze, leathery chest had a sheen on it that glinted like blood. His clothes were in a suitcase under the bed. In the morning he'd probably be white again, get dressed and light his pipe and flirt with the girls, forgetting that he'd ever been up on the rez scaring the hell out of the Indian children.

There wasn't anything else to do but wait. Priest was almost out the door when

Gramps whispered, "Give me your blade." Then he muttered something else in Apache.

Priest looked down.

He was holding his knife, blazing insanely in the moonlight and in his mind.

No use fighting it any longer. The images caught up with him and kicked around the inside of his skull, and it was better letting them in than it had been fighting to keep them out.

Priest wasn't sure why he wanted to be alone with Deed. Why he wanted him and Lamarr to be left alone with Deed and his pards, but for some reason it was important even if it made the job harder. Since the day that the hulking Wainwright had become houseman, he'd never left his post. He'd never taken a vacation or asked for time off or not shown up when he was supposed to. Priest wanted him to leave now.

And Patty, too. Downstairs later he kept looking across the table at her, and she at him. She'd suddenly quit avoiding his eyes, giving it to him long and slow, top to bottom. Their gazes locked and tangled and even fluttered aside like those of new and former lovers will do. Perhaps they were both embarrassed by feelings and events that were already seven or eight years gone. He couldn't shake off the sense that his ego, in some way, had been wounded, though he couldn't figure out how. Before today he hadn't thought he had much pride left anymore, but there it was.

The tension kept growing, and the usual frenzy and pain were almost comforting in a way. It calmed him down further. He really would have to dwell on that some and try harder to avert the madness that ran in his blood.

In the meantime he decided to let it go. He turned to Wainwright and said, "I want you to take her upstairs."

"Now, wait a damn minute," Patty protested. "Who do you think you are to talk to me like that in my own house?"

Wainwright had heard everything and understood it all. "Certainly. If you need any help, just holler."

"Sure."

Priest was again amazed that a man who looked so much like an animal could be so clear in his thinking. Wainwright knew bloodshed was coming, and it was his foremost duty to protect Miss Patty and the ladies. As a friend, he allowed Priest to follow his course.

"You want I should go, too?" Lamarr asked, trying to be helpful. "I fear Lorelei ain't being quite as satisfied as she might be, that poor darlin'."

"Are you men talking about me as if I'm not here?" Miss Patty asked, her voice breaking down the middle. "You got the gumption for that?" She grabbed the neck of the rum bottle until her knuckles cracked, ready to smash it into somebody's nose. "I've got to say that you boys have shown me a fair amount of discourtesy so far today. I reckon I won't put up with any more of it."

Priest stood and she did, too. Patty stepped closer, her shoulders dappled with sweat. She brought her lips nearer, and nearer still until he almost leaned in toward her expecting that familiar taste again. That's how it was, once.

She flashed him those dimples that, as always, made his entrails buck. He spun to one side hoping she didn't notice how he flinched.

"Go upstairs."

"This is my place, Priest McClaren. Nobody tells me what to do in it."

They could go around like this for a couple of hours, but Priest didn't have it in him. "Just go," he said.

"Why?"

"I've got a thing or two I'd like to talk to Deed about."

"His real name isn't Deed, it's—"

"I don't care."

She touched the side of his face, and he turned his mouth to her palm but didn't kiss it. "You pick the damnedest times to play the fanciful romantic, you headstrong fool."

"Go on."

Priest thought about it for a moment and realized it was true. He wanted to add something but there wasn't anything else to say, so he simply watched as she stormed up the steps followed by Wainwright, whose bulk filled the stairway and blotted out the lamplight.

Lamarr and Priest sat in the parlor, playing cards. Three stragglers wandered in over the course of the next hour, all pretty drunk, and Priest didn't need to do much more than turn them around and give them a push to set them back on their way again.

Someone directly overhead on the second floor let out a high-pitched cry of jubilation that surged into a shriek. It sounded very painful.

Lamarr said, "That'd be the right proper work of Lorelei we're hearing."

"Any chance that banker she's with will live through the night?"

81

"Don't think she's lost one yet. But it'll take an ax handle to beat the smile off that jasper's face tomorrow. She got natural God-given talent, Lorelei does."

The banker let out another shrill squeal that was met by an undulating feminine scream. The screeching went on like that for a while until it made Priest wince.

"She sounds pretty satisfied to me," he said.

"Goddamn. And here I was feelin' sorry for her."

"I've got a question."

"No," Lamarr told him. "I ain't never got her to make that there noise, and there's no need to rub my nose in it."

"That's not my question."

"Oh, well, all right then."

"Why do you carry a Confederate gun?" Priest asked.

"I'm from Georgia, after all."

"You fought for the Union."

"Well, I was a slave, too."

"I haven't forgotten."

"Neither have I." Lamarr drew his revolver and handed it to Priest.

Although it had been converted, the pistol was a real 1851 Navy .36 and not one of the Southern Navy revolvers with brass components produced by the Confederacy when steel became hard to obtain. It was light, less than three pounds, and well balanced. It was the first time Priest had ever held the gun, and he enjoyed how it sat in his hand. No wonder it was the most common model used during the war. Southern arms manufacturers copied them more easily than the .44.

"Cavalry horsemen favored it," Lamarr said. "Worn by General George Custer hisself."

"Didn't help him much at Little Bighorn."

"I reckon I won't argue that particular point. Also worn by the prince of pistoleers, ole Wild Bill. He never did convert to cartridge though."

Priest almost didn't want to let the gun go, but he handed it back as the aggressive noise of heavy boot steps filled the porch.

Deed came with his pards. Two hardcases in almost the exact same serge frock coats and brocade vests, carrying Bibles and strapped with pistols, also playing the preacher game but nowhere near as good as Deed did. It was now dark enough that they could come to the house without arousing any real suspicion from the rest of the town.

They fanned out and silently checked the alcoves and peered up the stairwell, ignoring Priest and Lamarr at the table. When they were satisfied there would be no ambush the three closed ranks again and approached.

Lamarr didn't drop his smile any but managed to glare at Deed with genuine hatred. "At least they ain't dressed like Spanish monks. Now that would've been just plain blasphemous."

"I don't talk to underlings," Deed said. "Call Patty down or I'll go look for her."

Priest went to the bar and got four glasses. He set the bottle of rum in the center of the table and handed out the glasses. "She's here, but you can deal with me for the moment."

"Like I told you—"

"Relax. Sit and have a toot first. Then we'll take care of business. If we can't struggle through to an understanding, then she can work out the finer details with you."

Deed considered the proposal and let it ride. He noticed Priest didn't have a glass and said, "You're not having one? I'd have to say that's mighty unfriendly of you."

"Don't take it personal," Priest told him. "I spent five years smelling like mash liquor and crawling naked through pig shit."

"It's true," Lamarr said, and it was. The first time they'd met had been when

Lamarr had pulled him out of a hog sty. "Even the pigs used to keep away from him. You never seen such scared sows."

Priest watched the three newcomers sit and drink. They were lookalikes. They had the same sort of hands—long, bony, and pale fingered. Deed kept hold of his Bible, tight to his chest, but the others had already put theirs down. All three had near-white blond hair worn way too short, cut with a dull straight razor, prison-style. They'd run together for so long that they'd taken on the same stern expressions and mannerisms, the same stink, the same jut of their chins. Major Gruber stood out a little more because of his age, maybe twenty years older than the other two, but the sun and chain gangs had pretty much evened them all out.

"Where's them sweet girls you been telling us about?" Longstreet asked.

"Busy, I hope," Deed said. "Making money."

Gruber had a saber scar that crawled out from beneath his collar and up to his left ear, surely a memento of his days riding under Bragg. By chance he'd sat beside Lamarr and it clearly bothered the hell out of him. Lamarr kept the smile eased out, really putting his spirit into it, even showing off his back teeth now. Gruber tried not to shy away as he frowned. "You in the war?"

A soldier could pick another soldier out of a room full of men. "For a fair while," Lamarr said.

"Kill lots of Rebs?"

"Only the ones who whistled Dixie at me."

"Let me tell you," Gruber said, facing into the brilliant white of Lamarr's smile. "My granddaddy was a plantation owner."

"That right?"

"Yep. Owned fifty slaves."

"That all?"

"They was the goddamnedest herd of niggers you ever done met. Animals, really. Some straight from Aferca."

"Never been there myself."

Gruber had a practiced glower and he tried to wither Lamarr with it. Gruber's breath hissed from his nose, with his canines clicking as he settled deeper in his seat. He kept the scowl going until the edges of his eyes began to water.

Lamarr continued beaming and said, "What was your granddaddy's name? Maybe I knew the man."

Lamarr was thinking about Thompson again, hearing in his head those sounds the master made as Lamarr choked him with his left fist and then his right.

"You know what the trouble with niggers is?" Gruber asked.

"I'd be beholden to you if you enlightened me."

"They don't know when they got it good."

"That might be true. When I used to get whipped and salted, I almost never realized how good I had it."

"Yep, that's the way of it." Gruber's scar seemed alive and separate from him, seeking purchase elsewhere.

"Bet you striped a black back or three in your time."

"To be sure I done that some, too. Right down to the bone."

"Enough of the good old days," Deed put in, leaning toward Priest. He still clutched the Bible tightly to himself, and Priest wondered what the real story there was. "Let's talk business. Patty and I are kin, the only kin we got left."

"That's important," Priest said, and he meant it.

"We're flesh and bone and blood. There isn't anything as important as that."

"I agree with you."

"She owes me and I'm here to collect what I've got due."

Priest knew a lot about the significance of family. But hearing Deed sound so sincere even while the greed dripped in his voice made Priest's scalp prickle.

"I'm coming back every week for half the house profits. She either pays me or I'll preach each day out front, all day long, and gather my congregation and drive her out of town."

"Seems to me blood wouldn't do that to blood."

"Don't you believe it."

Priest tried not to sigh. "I reckon I don't, really."

"If she doesn't give me what I want then my righteous wrath will descend on this house."

Priest's hand flashed out. He grabbed the Bible so quickly that Deed continued to hold his hand to his chest as if he were still carrying the book. It wasn't until Priest flicked through the pages that Deed realized it was gone.

You made your play when you had to do it, and you followed through to the end. Deed thrust his seat from the table and sat there blinking and sort of growling. His pards joined in. Gruber and Longstreet drew their guns on Priest and Lamarr, who waited calmly. Gruber carried a Smith & Wesson .38 pocket model. Longstreet held an ugly little revolver that looked hammered together from junk.

"What in blazes kind of gun is this here thing?" Lamarr asked.

Longstreet didn't answer, so Priest said, "It's a Pepperbox."

He'd seen one before, when he was a kid. A .31 five-shot revolving percussion Pepperbox pistol. It had five tightly-ringed rifled barrels, with a ring cocking trigger lever and a separate trigger for firing. All five barrels pulled forward on a hinged breech. The walnut grips had an engraved floral scroll like the opening pages of a book of poetry. It was a screw-barrel pistol, much more powerful than muzzle-loading ones. It looked like the kind of pistol snappy civilians would favor until it blew up in their hands. It was a stupid gun for stupid men.

Gruber held the .38 almost to Lamarr's temple. "I could put a bullet in your eye but I'd rather see you swing from a tree. That's what we do with uppity niggers where I come from."

"Well, I come from that same place, and I s'pect you ain't seen nary any uppitiness yet."

Deed's swivel holster was greased but he hadn't used it in a while. There was a tiny squeak as he moved it on his hip, aiming under the black-lacquer table at Priest's belly. He was so certain the trick would work that he reclined a little lazily in the seat now, stretching out.

Overhead, another cry undulated, keening wildly like a vulture's screech. The banker must've woken up and still been randy enough for another go. Lorelei moaned and wailed herself, making some heart-wrenching sobs.

"What in God's name is that?" Longstreet asked.

Lamarr turned to Priest and said, "Damn, maybe the poor bastard ain't gonna make it till mornin'. That Lorelei, sometimes she don't know when to stop."

"Maybe you ought to be glad you never got her to make that noise," Priest said. "Sounds like it could be one's undoing."

"She got this little wriggle she uses."

"That right?"

"It is. She sorta gets snaky."

"It saddens my soul to learn I might've gone my whole life without knowing that fact."

"Shut up!" Gruber shouted. "You two get on your knees and crawl! When that whore finds what's left of you she'll know not to fool with us no more."

"It's just a cheap show!" Longstreet said. He kept looking toward the ceiling. "They're scairt! It's a trick. There's gotta be somebody else here watchin' us."

"That'd be baby Jesus," Lamarr said. "And he don't like what he sees."

Priest said, "You three can leave town and play your game elsewhere. If you go now."

"It's no game for me," Deed said, grinning with such deep damage and hatred that Priest knew the answer to this puzzle was going to be supremely ugly. "Nor for you, son."

"That's right."

"You got the hurt look of a man who comes home and finds out his wife's been keeping the bed warm with somebody else. Patty owns a cathouse—what've you been thinking, that she's got a lily-white, pure heart?" Deed let out the venom, seething, spewing it, "You want to know, don't you? You got suspicions but you want me to say it, don't you?"

"No," Priest said.

"Well, I'll tell you anyways—I had her! I had her good. I was her first. Long before you, boy! So I took her in a shed when she was twelve, and she still would've been set on this course. I started her on her way, that's all, and you helped her further along down the path."

Those cloudy eyes lit with that lightning once more. Maybe it was lunacy, maybe just a reflection off one of the pistols.

But Priest understood with an intense clarity that he had to kill Deed. It sharpened his vision to such an extent that he felt as if the world had abruptly gone black and white.

Priest felt the moment coming, but he had to wait for Gruber to move his pistol from Lamarr's head.

Lamarr knew he had to do something and said to Gruber, "If you're really set on a lynching, I got some rope out back. Wait here and I'll go get it." He stood and Gruber actually did a little hop to get out of the way.

And there it was.

The trick shot was nothing without surprise. Priest hurled the Bible at Deed's face. The book caught Deed flush in the nose and sent him falling over backward in his chair. He managed to get off a shot with the Schofield but Priest was already gone. Longstreet had been looking at the ceiling, listening to the cries, and only now lowered his eyes. Gruber didn't know who to watch anymore and hesitated in pointing the Smith & Wesson. Lamarr drew both of his Navy .36s from his sash and fired directly into each of Gruber's thighs.

Blood arched and sailed across the table. Longstreet was coming around, aiming the Pepperbox at Priest's chest. That was all right. Priest had the knife out and held it by the blade, swinging the butt down into the hinged breech of the Pepperbox. He struck it as hard as he could.

All five shots went off at once in a tinny burst of metal and smoke. Longstreet screamed as the shrapnel tore his fist wide open and blew off two of his fingers. He took one look at the shards of burst knuckle bone sticking up through his flesh and passed out.

Deed wanted to take another shot from the floor but he couldn't get the swivel to swing to the correct angle, and he'd played the trick for so long that he didn't even think of actually drawing the gun. Gruber thrashed in agony and rolled over the preacher, leaking and splashing blood everywhere.

Lamarr said, "See there, Major. Now that's uppity!"

Whatever else he might be missing, Gruber didn't lack for scorn. He managed to swallow down enough of the pain to get some words out. "You're a damn fool, nigger," Gruber said. "If you don't kill me I'll just keep coming back, and one of them times I'll get you on the hanging tree! And I'll be whistling goddamn Dixie when I do it!"

"The nasty fact is that I do believe you, Major," Lamarr said, and shot him in the head.

Deed took it in stride, perhaps the way a man who actually believes in heaven might. He stood and didn't bother to glance at his fallen pards. He kicked the Bible aside and it tumbled toward Priest, who picked it up.

Deed sneered until his upper lip almost sealed his nostrils. "I want to see Patty."

"Sorry, Cousin Josiah," Priest said. "But she doesn't want to see you."

"I'll get what's mine!"

"Sure."

"I shall be—"

"Go away now or it's going to go bad."

"That's the only way it can be, boy!"

They looked up together to see a shadow unfurling from the darkness at the head of the stairs, rising now and lunging forward.

Gramps gave a coyote wail war cry. He came down the steps three at a time and snarled at Priest in Apache. Priest had a pretty good idea what Gramps wanted. He flipped the knife up, and the old man caught it in midair as he leaped upon Deed. The preacher let out a cry to God and hit the floor hard, with Gramps crouched over him grunting and wheezing, as the blade wove gently against the flesh of his throat.

They waited like that for a while. Finally Deed whispered through his clenched teeth, "What's this crazy bastard want?"

Priest said, "I think he's mad that you tried to get rid of his *Ga'ns* spirits. Or maybe it's just the spirits themselves that are awful angry."

"Jesus, you're as sick in the head as he is!"

"Maybe you should apologize to him and the mountain ghosts."

"You and your ghosts can all go to hell."

Gramps backed away, gesturing with his hands. He even pointed at Lamarr, who had tossed his guns on the table and sat there drinking with his feet up. Like Lamarr, Gramps or the spirits had decided to leave whatever vengeance was left to Priest.

Deed understood it, too, and chuckled as he got up and brushed himself off. Here he was, facing a man who had no weapon. Over there, a buck drinking in a chair without his guns. An insane, naked old man barking and yelping.

There was righteous wrath to be had.

Deed spun the long-barreled pistol in its swivel holster.

Everything unfolded almost the same as before, everybody pitching objects around the room, as if this had been practiced many times previously. Priest hurled the Bible again in the same instant that Gramps threw him the knife.

The book flapped open as it hit Deed's chest, and the soft crinkling of pages was like a whisper of forgiveness in the night. The book wasn't open to the center, but further toward the back where the New Testament taught absolution and mercy, none of that eye for an eye.

Time was running out already, the book about to fall, the open-ended holster angling up toward Priest's belly. The black mouth of the barrel appeared through the bottom of the leather.

Priest remembered his mother's prayers, the eulogy for Patty's father, the lectures and brimstone accusations, and the torrent of grief that followed him into and out of church. The book was moving now, beginning to drop. Deed's lips started to creep, maybe into a smile, maybe not. Priest didn't really care.

He drove the blade cleanly through the Bible, and continued to thrust it deep into Deed's heart.

* * *

Five days later, Patty found him preaching in a hog pen to a sounder of pigs about to be butchered.

Wainwright carried him back to the house and put him to bed upstairs in Gramps's room. Patty stayed with him the entire time, wiping sweat out of his eyes, spoon-feeding him stew, and cleaning up his mess until he could keep some food down. He barely remembered talking to the sheriff or spending a couple of nights in jail until he'd been cleared.

Gramps came to visit him once at the shack, dressed in a nice suit with a bow tie and suspenders, smoking his pipe. They didn't talk about much, and wound up just sitting there enjoying each other's company for a bit.

After another full day in bed Priest still hadn't completely dried out. He awoke late in the night, the room almost completely dark, and Patty was there beside him.

"There wasn't a reason in the world for you to have done what you did," she said.

He didn't know if she meant killing Deed or preaching to the pigs, so he kept quiet.

"You don't love me, you know. Not anymore."

Priest's voice was still raw from the

whiskey, and he didn't recognize it as his own. "You and I, we're as good as blood."

"Yes."

"That's all that matters then. The rest—it'll sort itself out or it won't."

"I heard him shouting. He told you terrible things. They were true, but they were awful."

"Worse for you than me."

"I'm not sure about that. I locked what happened—what he did—away from me. You couldn't."

"No."

She whirled away then, her petticoats flapping, her hair a jumble of shadow in a deeper darkness. He heard the tears falling from her chin and striking the floor. As she drifted out the door she said, "Thank you."

It wasn't until he threw the sheets aside that he realized she'd laid a Bible on his pillow, alongside his knife. He picked them both up, weighing each carefully, one in each hand, and stayed like that until the sun's rays began to light up the pages, and the edge of the blade shone back at him with his own bitter face.

Chapter Six

The next afternoon he went to see his sister Molly and her four-month-old daughter, Katie, named for their late mother.

She had bought a house over on Broad Street, directly across from Freerson's Dry Goods Emporium, thinking it might stop Gramps from slipping out when he went Apache—all the other old men sat in front of the store most of the day, chewing and spitting and telling their tales as they sat in their rocking chairs, commenting on fat women's asses.

But Gramps still managed to escape just fine anyway.

At the moment he stood out on the porch, looking toward the mountains, already starting to lose some of his tenuous hold on the white world. His bow tie was loosely knotted and one of his suspenders had come free. The pipe jutted from the corner of his mouth but wasn't lit.

Gramps barely acknowledged Priest as he came up the steps. A gray hand reached out and firmly gripped his shoulder, as if holding on for another minute, and then loosened and fell away. Priest decided not to disturb his grandfather as the old man waited, poised at that cliff's edge in his own head, and began to cross over it. Chicorah was going to have his hands full soon.

Priest opened the screen door, walked inside, and said, "Hello?" Prickly pear blossoms coursed in alongside his ankles.

"In the kitchen," Molly called, her childlike voice filled with a singsong quality. It did him good and began to lighten his mood. He imagined how she must've yodeled and crooned when she traversed the plains and the mountains, making lonely camps along the gallows land.

She still had plenty of guns around the place and the house smelled of powder. Priest found her jacket hung over a ladder-back chair and noticed the flash burns at her cuffs. He sniffed at it and his eyes watered—she was still practicing.

Half a decade ago, Priest and Molly had

been forced to watch the murder of their parents at the hands of Spider Rafe and Yuma Dean. They never talked of it openly, not once, and he was pondering on if it might help—either her or him—to do so after all this time.

Though Molly had managed to unload their daddy's Colt .45 pistol into Rafe's chest and save Priest's life, Yuma Dean had turned tail and kept on the loose. Molly, who hadn't quite been thirteen yet, had the damnable McClaren insanity burning inside her and went on the prod, an adolescent girl quickly making a name for herself as a bounty hunter. Priest became a drunkard until Lamarr helped him out of the bottle.

On the night Katie was born, Priest had finally met up with Yuma Dean again and killed him out at Septemus's hacienda. It hadn't cleared his mind as much as he'd been hoping.

Both Molly and Priest needed to figure out what to do with their lives now that the raw need for revenge had been appeased, if not altogether satisfied. He wondered if it would ever really be over.

Splashing sounds grew louder as Priest stepped into the kitchen. Molly was giving the baby a bath in a porcelain basin, the bubbles piled atop Katie's head and climbing halfway up Molly's arms.

"She's rabid!" Priest said.

"You'd think so, the way she hates water."

His sister's high cheeks, burned from years on the trail, would always be a bright shade of red. She had full pink lips set in a sun-browned face, and some of the golden color was returning to her bleached hair after settling in Patience a few months back. Her natural curls draped past her shoulders, the wet ends dampening her shirt. Those blue eyes remained slightly cold but they had warmed considerably since Katie's arrival. Their mother's beauty resided in the softness of her heart-shaped face, another ghost in the angles and dimples.

"I'll be done in only a few minutes."

"Let me," he told her, and took over bathing the baby. Katie stared at him in terror, grimaced, and let out a deep sigh of discontent.

"Be careful to hold her up, she can't sit on her own yet."

"I know."

"Don't get soap in her eyes."

"I won't."

"Watch her neck."

"I'm watching."

Katie's features had started to fill out and there was a cheerful roundness to her now as her personality began to form and show through. An intense curiosity had already gripped the infant. She stared at Priest and brought her tiny fists up to his chin while he used the washcloth to wipe her down. He carefully cleaned the thick, coarse hair that hadn't fallen out yet, the way he'd heard it was supposed to do.

"You had quite a week," Molly said. "I visited you in jail. Don't suppose you recall."

"No."

"You were busy quoting Scripture."

"Was I?"

"Yeah. I was surprised that you still remembered so many of the passages Pa taught us."

Priest frowned and Katie reached for his eyebrows, nabbing a few hairs. He tried to think of a single verse from the Bible and couldn't come up with any.

He realized that the other man he could sometimes become often knew a great deal more than he did himself, and it frightened him.

"I spent a bit of time behind bars in cells just like that one," his sister said in a hard tone.

He turned to look at her and Katie nearly pulled his face off. "You did?"

"Yep. Put there by men just as ignorant and arrogant as Sheriff Amos Burke. And filled with that same sort of swaggering pride to make up for their stupidity. Scamps who cared more about their mustaches and their horses than they did people or the law. Half of them were middling fat jaspers who had to carry shotguns because they couldn't get their gun belts around their bellies anymore. Most of them are dead now."

"You take care of 'em?"

"Some." She wagged her fingers like she was warming up for a gunfight. "Those who deserved it."

"'Pride goeth before destruction, and a haughty spirit before a fall.'" There, that was one.

"And a swagger doesn't do much against a real desperado."

"No, I don't suppose it would. But I don't hold it against Burke. He was just doing his job. I was the fool."

"You were in pain, there's a difference."

Sometimes it didn't feel like there was any. Priest dried the baby off, dressed her, and put her down in the crib where she immediately fell asleep. Molly walked with him to the sitting room and they both took seats facing one another, the silence growing peaked, getting a bit sharp.

They still didn't know each other very

well, and there remained that air of anxiety and uneasiness between them. A lot of blood and whiskey had flowed in those five years they were away from one another, and they hadn't quite figured out how to bridge the distance from his shore to hers yet. Lamarr had told him to just let it be, but Priest couldn't shake the feeling that somehow time was running out for them.

"If you ever need help, you can always come to me," she said. "I hope you understand that."

He knew she was talking about killing.

Molly had made a small fortune hunting wanted men, and had given up nearly all of her youth in pursuit of Yuma Dean because Priest couldn't handle the blood debt at the time. He figured that she still had to hate him for it, whether she admitted it or not.

"Thanks," he said, "I'll keep it in mind."

"You don't need to feel guilty over a bunch of bastards like that. I ran across Foley Longstreet in Nacogdoches a couple of years back. He's lucky he lasted as long as he did, playing around with a goddamn Pepperbox."

"What do you mean 'ran across'?"

"That doesn't matter. He was trash and so were the others he ran with. You shouldn't let what happened to them throw you back into the hog pens. There are plenty of folks who'll make a pilgrimage to spit on their graves."

A mesquite-laced breeze swept through the house. It flowed down his collar to rub his chest like the hand of a loving woman. Molly gave him a grin that he couldn't read. They'd always have secrets from one another, but the wealth of them occasionally surprised him.

"You hungry?" she asked.

"Yes," Priest said though he wasn't. Maybe a meal would break the conversation down into something manageable.

She still cooked as if she was on the trail. Beans, bacon, corned beef, and boiling coffee, and she served it all on tin plates as if she might need to pack them in her saddlebags at any minute.

"He's about to go off again," she said. "Gramps."

"Yes."

"I'm almost getting used to it."

"Might as well, there's nothing we can do about it."

"I thought that with the baby here—"

Priest had thought the same thing. That having a child in the house might help the old man to keep focused on his kin, but maybe the *Ga'ns* spirits were just too strong. "He considers them to be family, too. Chicorah's people."

"He's not so torn as that. He'd rather be on White Mountain."

"It's not us he's getting away from."

"I know, but I still miss him." She didn't use silverware to eat with, instead mopping the plate with thick pieces of stale bread. "Someday Sub-chief Sondeyka is going to have to order his bucks not to let the old man on the rez anymore."

"No, he won't."

"It's a matter of principle. The Apaches aren't allowed off the reservation; he can't allow white men up onto the mountain."

"Gramps isn't white when he goes there. When he starts turning back into a pale eyes, that's when Chicorah will return him to town. He's considered a holy traveler to them."

"So are you from what I hear tell. Chicorah thinks you're possessed by those same spirits, too."

"Yep."

Priest ate slowly and felt oddly relaxed, sated in a way he didn't like. Her childish, high voice was gentle as a lullaby, and gave him the sense of being wrapped in his sister's soft arms, the same way their father's music had pressed like a cool rag against Priest's fevers when he was a child. He

107

kept seeing their mother's face in Molly's, but the harder he searched the faster Ma drifted away.

Their father, Dr. Preach McClaren, didn't know why the music worked when the medicines didn't, but he was thankful for it. He played all the time even though Ma was deaf. She'd rosin his bow, hand it to him, and occasionally lay out sheet music so he could attempt some classical pieces. She liked how everyone smiled. Molly would sit on her lap so that Ma could look at the side of her face and watch her laughing.

The swell of the past was almost strong enough to make him reel. Did Lamarr ever work himself up like this, thinking of the morning he strangled the plantation master? Those years as a runaway slave, then in the army, and afterward hunting Septemus? How did he stay so fiercely in control?

Priest stood quickly, forcing himself to breathe normally, feeling half-witted and weak. Gramps looked in through the screen door, crazy but perceptive enough to know when Priest was standing on the same ledge. Were they both bound to run around naked on White Mountain grunting in Apache, scaring hell out of the children?

"You going?" she asked.

"I ought to be."

Molly tried to keep the disappointment out of her face but didn't quite manage it. She let you know exactly what she thought, always—it saved on confusion later. She wanted Priest to be as strong as she was, someone she could depend on when it mattered most, like she might trust her trigger finger or her best Colt .45. He was already failing her.

But she had picked up a few social graces since returning to town and tried to slick over the trouble patch. "I still haven't gotten around to buying much furniture for the house."

"Oh?"

"I was thinking of doing some shopping this afternoon, pick up a few more needed odds and ends. I have a cradle but still no crib yet for Katie. Feel like coming along?"

"I'd like to but I have something important I need to do."

"What's that?"

It was time to go see Sarah.

Priest turned to leave. Gramps was already gone by the time he hit the porch.

Storm clouds surged and sheet lightning wove through the vault of the sky to the west. He rode out across the foothills toward Septemus's hacienda as fat raindrops started to slash down, icy and stinging. They snapped against his back like lashes from a salted whip.

What the hell was he doing? He pulled his hat lower and kept scanning the foothills, waiting for Lamarr to come bolting out of the brush, laughing that Priest thought he could actually hide something from him.

Even from a half mile off you could make out the ornate gate that stood closed before the Hart ranch. A couple of sentries spotted him, but they didn't ride to meet and brace him.

Thunder burst and echoed so loudly that for an instant Priest thought they were lobbing sticks of dynamite. He urged the roan on faster and the freezing wind slapped and numbed his skin.

The storm unleashed itself completely and a wall of rain came down so thick that his horse stopped as if they'd hit a barricade. Priest's teeth hurt and he didn't know why until he realized he was smiling. He looked down and was relieved to see that the knife wasn't in his right hand.

He relaxed in the saddle for a second until he noticed the wet blade in his left fist instead.

Okay, so it was going to be like that.

The skittish roan whinnied in fear as it

grudgingly moved ahead again, picking up speed until it raced across the flooding gullies and fought through torrents of swelling mudslides. Priest kept a tight hold on the reins, trying not to think about how the *Ga'ns* spirits appeared to be angry because he was riding to aid some of the people who'd helped destroy Apacheria.

Lightning ignited on top of him and the thunderclaps erupted so close together that the roaring crashes seemed like one continuous bellow. He almost liked the sound of the world rising up against him.

Priest drew up to the gate and a drenched, grizzled face appeared on the other side, staring warily into the dark gloom of the squall. "You McClaren?"

"Yeah!"

They both had to shout. "I'm Merullo, the new foreman!"

Priest waited. Merullo stood in the onslaught wearing an open duster and a ten-gallon hat with water pouring off the brim, hands loose at his sides. The electrified air grew a little more agitated with unsaid words. Priest wondered if Merullo would mention Cobb, the former honcho whom Lamarr had killed the last time they were here. He cocked his head as the heaving wind burst across his back.

Your past followed you into the day, and

sometimes even beat you to where you were going. Merullo decided to play it smart and let the moment pass. He said, "The boys will lead you to the main house! Mrs. Hart is waiting for you!"

He swung open the gate and Priest rode on toward the rancheria, a couple of the other men falling in beside him as escorts. He glanced down and saw that he'd sheathed the knife.

Septemus had been busy the past few months rebuilding the hacienda. The main house, barracks, and other outer buildings had all been damaged back when Priest had caught up with Yuma Dean, and the Apaches attacked the ranch, but you couldn't even tell now. Everything had been completely restored.

At the house he dismounted, expecting the others to usher him inside. They didn't, and he wound up just standing there, unsure of the etiquette. The front door had been replaced, too.

He knocked gently, curious to see if Septemus himself would answer.

A Mexican handmaid opened the door and without a word led Priest through the corridors and out back, where Sarah stood in the gardened piazza, staring into the storm. She looked toward the smaller replica of the Home Hearth Theater that

Septemus had built on his land for her, perhaps to always remind Sarah of the playhouse where she'd made a name for herself as a singer before she'd married him.

Priest imagined her in there late at night, when the moonlight drifted so low and bright that you could run your hands through the silver, and she'd be singing only for Septemus. The little bastard sitting up in the balcony in his high seat of honor, sipping sherry and dressed in black trousers with a purple shirt, wearing his gray rebel coat with gold epaulets, all the medals on it reflecting the flickering stage lights. He was the only person allowed to hear her songs now, this master of the estate, and Priest counted that as just one more slight the man had done him.

She turned those grave eyes on Priest again, and he still couldn't make out exactly what was going on inside her head. She said, "Ye'll catch yer death."

The damp curls of her black hair lay heavily against her cheeks. Her face remained ashen, and the dark marks under her exhausted eyes had deepened further until they appeared to be incisions.

"What's he done to you?" Priest asked.

Her pursed lips parted and he shut his eyes hoping to hear a lengthy inventory of Septemus Hart's sins.

"My—"

"What is it, Sarah?"

"My husband—"

She groped for the words, damn near paralyzed with forcing herself to say them. He chewed his tongue until he tasted tartness. Priest would kill Septemus in that balcony, toss each one of the medals down to the shadowed seats below, and then sit in his chair and slowly finish the man's sherry.

He reached out and ran the back of his hand against the line of her jaw, feeling the soft blond down there beneath her ears. Their dead child's voice told him to wait and listen, hear her out before passing judgment. But Priest could feel the thrum of thunder in his heart, pressing him forward into the house, where he'd begin his hunt for Septemus Hart.

Finally she managed to cough the words clear as she broke into sobs. "My husband . . ."

"What?"

". . . has been . . ."

"What!"

". . . kidnapped!"

The *Ga'ns* spirits began to waft off and the storm eased around the house. Wind and rain abated within seconds, or at least it felt that way. Priest licked his lips and tried to hold it down but just couldn't help himself. He snorted once and then burst out laughing.

"Priest McClaren!"

The guffaws boiled up from him until he thought he might be sick right there on the fine Mexican tiles. He shook and held his belly and the tears squirted from his eyes. This is what they did in the madhouses, of course, when they couldn't control themselves any longer.

When he was finally able to look back at Sarah, trying to grin and maybe be a little charming like in the old days, she hauled off and punched him in the face.

Priest fell back a step and blood ran across his teeth.

"Ye'll not laugh about this!"

There it was. The child told him to put down the knife and he twisted aside, bringing the back of his hand up to his mouth, praying the kid was wrong and he wasn't holding the blade. Control, he had to exert control. He couldn't be doing something this crazy and deadly, not against her. Jesus, even the spirits were cackling at him.

Priest turned slowly, making sure his hands were empty. Sarah stood trembling, coils of hair bobbing across her forehead, the muscles in her jaw tight and, he could see, throbbing. More thunder rumbled distantly, low and almost quiet, like the titters of a lynch mob.

"Who in the hell would want to kidnap him?" he asked.

The anger drained out of her so quickly that she nearly collapsed. She paled in an instant, shoulders abruptly sagging, and she stumbled. Priest moved to catch her before she hit the ground, wanting to draw her near and also wanting to run, as blood ran down his throat.

"It's all right, Sarah. I'm here." That was his father's voice now, coming out of him.

Priest carried her to the lounge and laid her upon a half dozen pillows. She took his hand and held it tightly and they stayed like that for a while, the steady breeze whisking through the house.

"Tell me," he said.

"Are ye sure yer willing to listen?"

"Yes."

"One of his former business partners, that's who the black scoundrel is. Don Luis Braulio."

So they were back to the man the padre had mentioned a week ago, ruler of the pueblo across the river, who rustled cattle and raided caravans and smuggled guns.

Who had gotten wealthy too quickly until it brought out the animal in him and his faceless vaqueros. Who swindled and murdered whoever stood up to him, including old ladies of no consequence.

She sat up and had to brace herself against the cushions with both hands. Priest looked around hoping to find one of the servants to bring her a shot of bourbon or tequila, which she enjoyed every so often.

Sarah gave a grim smile, set herself, and continued. "In one of their livestock deals Don Braulio became very wealthy and now his standing's gone to his head. He's raising an army, exploiting his people, and he's become a competitor and rival rather than an associate."

"His standing?"

"He's the headman of a savage band, that one. Still, Septemus thought they remained on friendly enough terms, and rode out to Braulio's pueblo village to complete some final transactions concerning the herds."

Priest swallowed hard. She was even beginning to sound like the short bastard.

Septemus had been quickly expanding the borders of Patience and putting up so many buildings that carpenters, mill men, and architects came from as far away as

New Hampshire looking for a chance to make better pay in a swelling city. He ran liquor and guns and whores along the border. Septemus ruled the Home Hearth well and kept it the kind of establishment they talked about in Virginia City, New York, and St. Louis. Europeans frequently showed up alongside Mexican politicians. If any jasper got too far out of his head, Septemus's housemen would escort him out into the alley, and not even rough him up. Courtly and cordial is how Septemus treated everybody most of the time, even Lamarr.

Maybe Don Braulio didn't get enough of the reverence and admiration he'd been after all his life. Or maybe Septemus had cheated him in one of the deals. It had to be guns and ammunition, not livestock. Priest figured Braulio was about the same size as Septemus, too, maybe five foot three, always staring up at the rest of the world and hating everybody in it for that.

"Uh-huh. So," Priest said, "it's nothing serious at all. Just two brats fighting over spare change, some head of cattle, and a few miles of desert. To blazes with them both." He moved past her and a thread of smoke broke against his chin. His wet clothes were steaming.

"Don Braulio wants a ransom. Twenty thousand in cash, he's stated."

"That's all? Septemus must carry that much in his back pockets."

"Don't ye make light o' this!"

Sometimes you had to, or you'd finish going crazy. "They wouldn't risk going to war with him over twenty thousand. Septemus has his own armed force of men, and more importantly, he's got political pull. In the States and Mexico as well. There's something else going on here."

"What do ye mean by that, I ask?"

"Why'd you make me wait over a week before saying anything about this?"

"I had instructions to do nothing until today."

"Why would Braulio do that?"

"I don't know. I've met him only once, and I didn't like what I saw." She stood and the familiar Irish grimness flashed back into her eyes. "I need you and Lamarr to get my husband back."

He knew that was coming, and, somehow, would've been further heartbroken if she hadn't expected it from him. "Lamarr? He'd just as soon help Braulio stake Septemus out on a hill of army ants."

"Ye know that's not true. He would never

119

allow anything to happen to Septemus. Lamarr's his son—"

"He's never stepped up to it."

"—and they've too much left unresolved between them."

"Well, finding out his daddy was dumped facedown in a dry wash would resolve plenty for him, believe me."

She set her fists squarely on her hips, posing angrily the way his mother used to do, but her brogue softened. "Septemus said if anything went wrong I should ask you both for help."

"What?"

"It's the truth. No matter what's gone on between us all, he holds you and Lamarr in high esteem."

"Don't bull me!"

"Perhaps yer the only two men in Patience he does respect. Priest McClaren, please . . . I need you."

The rage came up in him so quickly that he doubled over and let loose a bark. The child's voice kept whispering, telling him to calm down, to open himself to the woman he probably still loved, and who had once loved him.

"Like hell!" he cried. "You just need someone to bring him back. You've got eighty hands out there on your payroll, why not send them after the little bastard?

That Merullo looks like he's handy with a gun."

"I can't trust any of those men!"

"You're damn right you can't, because Septemus hires only scum to work and protect his property. This is a ranch full of cutthroats, your husband being the worst!" His mouth overflowed with more curses, and he spit them out like a back-alley tomcat.

He went on for a few minutes like that, letting the fury fill and drain and then fill him again. At the end he stood heaving for breath, scowled at her, and said, "And what makes you think you can trust me, Sarah Hart?"

"Because you're my friend." She rested a hand on his arm and he snapped away as if struck by a snake.

"I might just as soon kill him as any Mexican bandit!"

"You would never do that to me."

"Don't be so sure of yourself, damn it!"

"It's you I'm certain about, Priest McClaren."

He didn't believe it. A week ago she had shrugged away from his touch, and now she was talking about friendship and devotion. He got the same feeling now as when Padre Villejo had first talked about this Don Braulio, as if someone were simply trying to put him to some use.

"When's the deadline?" he asked.

"In fifteen days."

"Where's the meeting?"

"At first it was Padre Villejo's mission, they said. And that's what I was doin' there. I'd never seen the place before and wanted to make sure I knew the location."

"And now?"

"Now he wants it brought to his stronghold."

"Well," Priest said without expression. "Well. How many vaqueros does Braulio have?"

"I'm not sure, but at least fifty men, I'd be expecting. He's promised safe passage to whoever carries the ransom."

"Why don't you set the mayor and sheriff on him? Aren't they Septemus's confidants?"

"The note said not to inform them or he'd be killed."

"How'd the first note arrive? Rider in the night?"

"Yes, who hurled it over the wall affixed to a dagger."

"Give it to me."

"Why?"

"Just do it."

She rummaged around in a drawer for a moment and returned with a scrap of paper with concise handwriting on it.

"Not that," Priest said, "the knife."

She left the room and returned five minutes later carrying a finely crafted blade. He took it and could immediately feel how much art and precision had gone into the weapon. This was the "slow knife" that Padre Villejo said Don Braulio liked to use against his enemies. He slipped it into his belt.

A flood of pain would follow, that much was clear.

Priest couldn't help chuckling, the scorn slithering inside him. She was so worried about her husband that she didn't much care she was sending Priest off to probably be dry-gulched. "Do you have the cash ready?"

"Yes."

"I have to talk to Lamarr about this."

"Of course. But ye already know what his answer will be."

Priest pictured Lamarr, his smile not nearly as wide as usual, thinking about Septemus dead in some arroyo in Mexico, never having admitted aloud that he was Lamarr's father. Ruminating on that for about a minute or so and going, "Daddy's still got some amends to make before he can go to his just reward."

Sarah stepped up close, arching her neck back as if she were about to kiss

Priest, perhaps one final time. He leaned in a few inches.

"There is one man who's loyal to Septemus," she said. "He'll help you in whatever capacity you need."

"A new gunny?" On that night, Molly had killed Septemus's left-handed gunny, Griff. Ever since, Priest had been waiting to hear about a new one standing grimly at his side.

"A personal bodyguard, yes. A man by the name of Hatcher Jowett."

"If he's so loyal, then why wasn't he with Septemus when he was taken?"

"Jowett is due to arrive from Vicksburg in two days. They've known each other since the war and are very close friends."

"Another Reb plantation owner?" Priest asked. "Oh, Lamarr's gonna love him."

Chapter Seven

There'd been a lightning strike in a stand of ash trees to the east of the valley, nearly on top of Lamarr's house. The flames still burned but the wind continued to press the fire toward the cliffs and desert terrain.

Lamarr lived just outside of town, on a hardscrabble patch in a solidly put-together shack he'd built himself. Clusters of thorny-stalked ocotillo brush framed the doorway. Down the newly cut road that crossed only a few hundred yards off, buckboards and coaches bustled by. Septemus had purchased plenty of the land surrounding the shack but he'd never make an offer to buy out Lamarr. Sometimes it was almost fun to see how they circled one another and got into each other's business without ever quite stepping over the line.

Priest wandered in and found Lamarr cleaning the .36s, his big yellow sombrero hanging off the back of his head. He was humming another one of his mother's slave songs, occasionally punctuating the tune with "Yes, Lawds." Priest sat at the table across from him and tried to figure out exactly how he was going to let out everything he had to tell.

He started twice and stopped, watching Lamarr's graceful, nimble fingers smoothly taking apart the guns, lovingly oiling and swabbing the parts. He tried again and once more nothing came out. Priest waited, knowing Lamarr would understand and gradually ease the conversation into motion.

The smell of burning wood drifted in, and a dark haze glided around the ceiling of the shack.

"Saw Molly and my beautiful niece in town today," Lamarr said. "Lookin' at some furniture in a shop window. Got herself one of them big grandfather clocks for the hallway of her house. She reckons that compared to Katie's young lungs it ain't so loud. Says Gramps hisself went off again."

"Yep."

"A little quicker than usual this time, ain't it?"

"If you want to call it usual."

He appeared to want to do so. "Seems the Apache life is just pullin' his heart into them mountains."

"Or his white life is pushing him."

Could that be it? Were Molly and the baby and Priest shoving the old man out of his skin instead of helping to hold him in place? Priest frowned, pondering it. The gathering of the family wasn't exactly doing wonders for his stability. Were Priest's escapades somehow harming his grandfather? Did all the mischief and misfortune, the pooling of McClaren blood and craziness, feed the *Ga'ns* spirits and allow them control over the old man?

"She also said you wasn't strictly in the best'a moods."

"Maybe not."

"You ain't got much of a positive disposition, but you still do manage some fine preachin' in a hog pen despite the fact. You got a little'a Jesus and his angels in you whether you like it or not."

"I think you might be right."

"Not a doubt in my head."

Lamarr had heard it for himself, the screaming fits behind the livery, Priest seeing the ghost of his mother flitting about him, her fingers tangling in his hair. He'd stumbled into a hog pen and would've been stomped to death if Lamarr hadn't gotten him out of there in time.

Mentioning the angels was Lamarr's way of inviting Priest to say everything he had to tell. So he did, letting it just run out of him as Lamarr deftly took his guns apart and put them together again. Speaking of a lost love could make a man hate his own voice, but the words sounded so much like the words of his father that he was almost comforted.

When he finished, Priest saw exactly what he expected to see. Lamarr's smile not quite as wide as usual, his eyes clouded with heavy musings as he thought about Septemus dead in some arroyo down in Mexico, never having admitted aloud that he was Lamarr's daddy.

He finally set aside the pistols. Ever since he'd made his run from the fields of Georgia, it had been his mission to look Septemus Hart in the eye and finally get recognized. You needed a greater purpose in life to give significance to the rest of your daily struggles.

Deliberating on it for another minute, Lamarr said, "They got a lot of slim and pretty women down there, that's for certain. *Mucho bonitas*. They ain't all carryin' an extra fifty pounds on their asses like some white men think."

"I admit, I was worrying about that there thing. Thanks for putting my mind at ease."

"I sensed it weighing on you." Now, he gave Priest the look, honest and deep but prankish, too. "You know, I don't much mind folks playing us for fools. Just wish it wouldn't happen so often."

"I have to agree."

Lamarr took up one of his guns again, snapped open the breach, shut it, cocked and then released the hammer. He'd never pull the trigger on an empty pistol. "We could always take the money and go see Fatima. She got some friends at the Bird Cage that would change your mood for the better. Twenty thousand will buy a fair amount of love."

"I'm up for it," Priest said. "Are you?"

Lamarr gave it considerable thought. "Well, I reckon I got more of a right to finish my own daddy off than some rich Mex bandit with a chip on his shoulder does. I don't like anybody steppin' in on my dance."

"Thought you might feel that way about it."

"Okay, so we go get Septemus back from

the Mexes. Guess we'll have to scout the premises, come up with a plan and all that shit."

"We're not too good at any of those considerations."

"No, it saddens me to agree, we're not. But we sure are hell at wingin' it. So far leastways."

"It's the first time we're not that worries me a touch."

Lamarr drew his chin back, giving Priest a long look-over, like he couldn't believe what he was hearing. "You fret too much."

"You think so?"

"I can see how you might let a few such small points trouble you on occasion. Like how when we cross the border we ain't gonna have us a whole wide world of friends waitin' to embrace us."

"I don't suppose you need to be reminded that we don't have a bushel full on this side of the river either."

"For somebody who's got a little'a Jesus and his angels in you, you sure ain't got much faith."

That stopped Priest and snapped him up in his seat a bit, but Lamarr didn't appear to notice and went on. "Chicorah and his men would help if we asked."

"Probably," Priest told him. "But last time he got a chance to shoot up all of

Septemus's men who were rousting the Apaches and raping their women. Now it would just cost him in bad relations. If the U.S. government officials got wind of it, his people would suffer."

"If you asked him to come, he would."

"I'm not asking."

Lamarr let out that grand white smile and, being who he was, said, "Good. Daddy's still got some amends to make 'fore he can go on to his justly reward."

Everyone did, in one way or another.

Priest sat back. "Let's go see Padre Villejo first. I'd like to hear more about the man who's got the pluck to kidnap Septemus Hart." He hoped they wouldn't walk in on another funeral.

Soft and breathy melodies swung across the flats. Sister Teresa and Sister Lorraina were tending the mission's garden, holding tightly to hoes with broken handles and chopping at the dry soil, trying to eke out a little more food six weeks after the harvest. They had their songs, Lamarr had his, and Sarah had hers. Priest wondered what his might be, and why he couldn't remember any.

A group of the orphan children were setting fire to a scorpion being attacked by a colony of black ants. The kids added sticks

131

and handfuls of dead grass on occasion, scrutinizing the scene in silence.

Padre Villejo sat off in the shade of a cluster of ash trees watching the children, his features trapped between sorrow, bitterness, and anger. He toyed with a large chunk of chalk, a stack of writing slates beside him. He taught English to the Indians and Mexicans who wanted to learn the language, though there weren't many.

It made you wonder what the whole fight was for. Padre Villejo hadn't left the mission in nearly ten years, and he looked like he was ready to leap up and crutch his way into town for a wild night in any saloon he could find. Spend a little time at Miss Patty's with Lorelei and get the chandeliers swinging. Who had the sand to tell him he didn't deserve it?

The kids had started to giggle and whisper as the fire they built grew higher. The burning scorpion tumbled out of the ring of flames and they prodded it back in with sticks. Crawling ants looked like a blazing puddle of oil spreading between them.

Two burros slept standing in the shade of a crumbling adobe wall near the trough. Priest and Lamarr dismounted and let their horses drink. Padre Villejo stared at them and his brow furrowed even more.

"Show some teeth, padre," Lamarr said.

"At least we ain't dripping blood on your floors this time."

"We must give thanks to God when we can, for whatever we can."

And begrudge Him the whole time, Priest thought. *Is that the lesson you learn burying bodies every day? When somebody can just come along and wander off with your leg?*

That piece of chalk went around and around in the padre's fingers, his jagged nails as white as if he'd crawled across the alkali barrens. He seemed to settle himself even deeper into his robes, the way the gunnies did when they were about to draw. "What brings you back to us when you are not bleeding?"

"We was hoping your cheerful disposition would rub off on us some," Lamarr told him. "We wanted to gladden our hearts with a bit of heaven."

Anybody else would think the huge ex-slave, ex-Union soldier might be trying to offend the padre, but Priest knew how much it hurt him to see a man of God losing his faith. Lamarr and his people had lived through just as much strife, and a whole lot worse, than that of the villagers. If Lamarr's mother could go to her grave praising Jesus after all she'd suffered on the plantation, then a man of the cloth who had his freedom could do no less.

133

"Is it so?" Padre Villejo asked.

"Yeah, it's so," Lamarr said. "No need to keep asking me that. If I say it, it's so. *Comprendes?*"

"We'd like to hear more about Braulio," Priest said.

Padre Villejo pulled a face and damn near chortled. The wooden cross around his waist bounced and clattered. Was he deliberately trying to insult them? It got distracting, the way the world worked around you most of the time, and forced you to lunge for the string and play it out however you could.

"And why do you ask this?"

"We're askin'," Lamarr said, "ain't that reason enough to answer?"

"Perhaps not."

"If I didn't know better, padre, I'd say you were purposefully being contrary."

"It is good that some know better than others."

Lamarr let out a sigh and pawed his chin, looking at the man from one angle and then moving aside a step, peering at him from another. "You protectin' him or us?"

"It is God who preserves and saves, not I."

"Appears He needs a little help then," Priest said, surprised at how upset he suddenly felt. His wrists ached with his pulse.

Maybe Deed had put him off all preachers of any ilk.

"That is blasphemy," the padre told him with no judgment in his voice whatsoever, the chunk of chalk still moving, weaving about smoothly. Maybe the man was finally losing his convictions.

Priest's hand flashed out and he nabbed the piece of chalk so fast that Padre Villejo's fingers continued moving for a moment as if he was still playing with it. He was startled to find it gone and he stared in surprise at Priest.

It was the meaningless signs that held the greatest importance. You went through life searching out importance in each useless action of every ill-considered man, and usually it meant only whatever you wanted it to mean.

But sometimes it was more, like this. The heft of the chalk reminded Priest of his own schooling days. Mama in front of the fireplace carefully spelling out words in cursive, the looping curls of her script something he could never quite duplicate.

He made a point of carefully putting down the piece of chalk on the top slate, showing that he could stay composed when it was needed. "Have you heard that Braulio's taken Septemus Hart hostage?"

That actually got a morose grin out of the padre. "God forgive me, this I would almost like to see."

"Me, too," Priest admitted.

"Hart is a corrupt tiny man with a small ill-tempered mind, who only pretends to be malevolent."

Lamarr chuckled and said, "He ain't exactly a sweet-smellin' daisy on the hill now, either."

"No, but he is nothing like Braulio."

"That right?"

"Hart is wealth and arrogance, but Braulio and his men are savagery and death to those who cross them."

There it was down on the plate, and Lamarr said, "Spending some time with Septemus might've given 'em a change of heart. They probably willin' to pay us twenty thousand to take him offa their hands by now."

Padre Villejo got back to frowning, his nervous hand staying away from the chalk and reaching down to touch the stump of his leg. "That's all Braulio asks?"

"Yep."

"He is too greedy to be satisfied with such a small amount from so rich a man. Lately, he has been leading strikes farther west and north, raiding villages and trying his hand against the railroad."

Priest said, "Last week you said his sudden wealth had brought out the beast in him."

"He's an outlaw, but his forces and their families grow larger every day. There's a price on his head. And . . . there are stories of what he likes to do to his enemies."

"Share some." Lamarr sat beside the padre, took off his sombrero, and hugged it to his belly looking like one of the orphan kids getting ready for a bedtime tale.

"Tell us about Donna Angelina Allasandro's son," Priest said.

"Orlando." The padre looked into their faces as if it might be the last time, still trying to make up his mind about how much to let out, giving them one last chance to back off before he said what he'd been eager to say. "Orlando fought against Braulio with a small band of comrades and was captured. Braulio makes his prisoners run across an open square for the far wall while he throws knives and machetes."

Priest still had the perfectly crafted blade in his belt. "He does it himself?"

"Yes, so it's told. He is proficient with these weapons, only a little less so with a pistol and rifle. He promises to release the captives if they can reach the wall and cross it alive."

Lamarr said, "I don't suppose we need to

wonder if he's a man of his word, that right?"

"He lets the bodies lie where they drop so the others must run over the corpses of their comrades, their brothers." Padre Villejo stared over at the children now, gazing into the flaming pile of insects. "Orlando and all the others died, except for one who made it over. Braulio kept his word and let him live, but he cut off the boy's feet first. Bound the wounds and set him on a burro."

"We might want to talk to him," Lamarr said.

"It is too late. After he recounted his story to us he cut his own throat so he would not be a burden to his family."

Reaching around so he could grip the handle of the knife, Priest found a strange solace in Braulio's weapon. "And you kept quiet? You never said anything about this before?"

That got the padre's blood up. It was good seeing him riled again, back in his natural state. "To whom? Your sheriff? You, *Preste*? Would you go to Braulio if your woman—the woman now lost to you—did not send you there for the sake of her own man?"

"You know about that?"

"As I said, it is good that some know better than others."

Not an admirable enough answer, Priest thought, when you were talking about Sarah and Septemus in the same breath. "When you take on a burden like that for yourself, you also take the responsibility."

"I know this."

Lamarr sensed where the argument was going and decided to stall it where it was. He stood, put on his sombrero, walked back to the horses, checked his saddle, and finally turned back. "You reckon there's any chance Septemus is still among the breathin', padre?"

"No, I do not believe so. Braulio has no reason to allow him to live. It is just more trouble for him. When the money is offered to him in exchange, he will steal it and kill those who bring it."

Wiping a trail of sweat from his cheek, Lamarr checked the sky, let out a fraction of his smile again. "Well, day's wastin'. I think after we finish down in Mexico way, we ought to stop over in Sonora. They got this little out-of-the-way place where the dancing girls line up together and sing songs in French. I don't know what the hell they sayin' but I like it anyways."

"You sure it's French?" Priest asked.

"It ain't English or Spanish."

"Okay, then it must be French."

"That's what I reckon."

Priest climbed onto his horse. "But don't think I've forgotten you still owe me from your other ventures."

"You accommodate me just another small loan and I'll pay you back everything plus a little extra for your generosity."

"Yeah, but will I still be young enough to spend it?"

"Your harsh words do my heart grave injury."

Padre Villejo looked at them the same way he had watched the children: uncertain of what he was witnessing, and whether he should be saddened or merely accepting of it. Where did a servant of God go when he'd lost his will to believe?

"You are courageous men, but your souls are dark, and sometimes I think you are the worst of fools."

"Maybe so," Priest said.

"Loving that woman, *Preste*, will bring you only suffering."

"I got my misery and you got yours," Priest said, yanking the reins and swinging his roan around. "I'll stake 'em up side by side anytime you like."

When they were about halfway back to town, the wind starting to come up and another storm brewing, Priest sensed eyes on him.

He stared off at the range, the distant brush, before he glanced aside and realized it was Lamarr watching him.

"That padre's a foul cuss at times," Lamarr said, fiddling with the brim of his sombrero. He really was worried about Septemus. "I don't think he trucks much with baby Jesus no more."

A little before dawn, Hatcher Jowett kicked open the door of Lamarr's shack, a snarl of disdain twisting his cracked lips as if he'd been lashed across the face. It didn't take much to set the mood of a new day.

Standing in the doorway, Jowett lifted his chin in the glow of the fireplace's embers, tongued one of his back teeth, and glanced around the small room. His gaze passed over Priest and Lamarr without taking notice. He wore gray pantaloons tucked inside of riding boots, and a canvas coat stiff up the back with dried mud. His sorrel drank loudly at the trough and stamped in agitation. The breeze grew heavy with the sweet scent of more approaching rain.

Jowett held a quirt weighted with a lead ball in the handle. Lamarr had once told Priest how some white masters would use braided whips and quirts to corral the slave women, chase them out of the fields and into the bedrooms. Maybe it's what Septemus had done to Lamarr's own mother, Lamarr had never said, but the room was quickly filling with the threat of murder. Priest stared over at the man and thought that somebody might just be dying or dead by the time the sun completely broke the horizon.

Still without a word, Jowett sat in one of the ladder-back chairs, took off his boots, and started knocking clumps of dirt from his heels against the table leg. When he finished, he drew a flask from his pocket and took a deep pull, then another, and one more before letting out a leisurely sigh.

He barely acknowledged Lamarr and said, "So, you're the nigger bastard who lays claim to be of Hart blood, that right?"

Lying on his bed, one hand out of sight beneath the pillow, Lamarr propped himself up on an elbow. "Why, you sweet-talkin' devil. You and Daddy both got them same well-bred social graces."

"Now don't sass me any, boy."

"Oh no, not me, suh."

"I'm already in a bad enough mood after riding into this desert purgatory, and I might decide to take it out on you."

"Shucks, please don't go doin' that, suh.

I got me enough worries in this wicked, burdensome world."

"I'd hazard a bold buck like you would."

"Uh-huh, yah." Lamarr lifted his head, grimaced, stretched the moment out and scratched at his temple. "But please, let me just say, suh, that those is some silly-ass lookin' pants you got on."

Priest smiled his first real smile in weeks.

Hatcher Jowett, in his late forties, hard muscled but compact and short legged, almost stumpy, didn't manage to hide his consternation. But at least he shut up before Lamarr drew his hidden Navy .36 and shot him in the forehead.

Both of them had gotten their opening licks in, which would hopefully be enough to keep them satisfied until daybreak.

Priest sat on the bunk across from Lamarr's bed taking stock of Jowett, noting the powder burn scars on his neck, the bad hip giving him some trouble. They had heard Jowett stumbling around in the clusters of thorny-stalked ocotillo brush a couple of minutes before he'd gotten to the door. The man wasn't much on finesse, and his ego got in the way of his own discretion. He'd underestimate everyone he had no respect for, and he obviously respected very few. Priest could tell Jowett was born into

143

the same standard of fortune, severity, and small-mindedness as Septemus. He had that same self-satisfied look about him. No wonder they were cohorts.

Jowett had covered part of the distance by stagecoach, but not the entire journey. The weather had bleached his already silvery hair and darkened and burned his skin. There were pink, raw patches on his forehead, nose, and cheeks, and he had some stinking glossy balm masking his face. Clearly, he hadn't been on the trail for a while, but he seemed proud and roused by his recent travels.

He'd lived most of his life on a horse before he started to feel the effects of his age. Though he'd taken to roving again he still had a bulging belly and swollen throat. His riding boots were dirty but Priest could see they were only recently bought and broken in. Jowett's mouth was thin and mean, and he enjoyed the slippery feel of his own complacent smirk.

Whatever the reason he was here, it wasn't only because he was friends with Septemus, and he wasn't a personal bodyguard, no matter what Sarah had been told. Some kind of debt was being paid, from one man to the other. Priest would watch and see if he could figure out which one of them was due.

"So you and Daddy is chums."

Jowett took a few seconds before deciding not to argue every time Lamarr called Septemus his daddy. There'd be time enough later to settle up on all the petty and trivial affronts.

With a grunt, Jowett said, "Septemus and I, we had us plenty'a good times down in Georgia and Mississippi and Louisiana."

"Figured you two weren't the kind to sit at home and ruminate."

"Not us."

"You come all this way to help him out of a rough patch, that so?"

"He and I . . . we got some unfinished business."

"Imagine that. Me and him, too. My daddy ain't much for finishin' business, so far's I can see."

"You know that, then you're smarter than I gave you credit for."

"Aw shucks, you just funnin' me now."

With a murmur, Jowett took another drink from his flask. He probably wasn't used to the rotgut you had to buy around here, and it was hitting him pretty hard. His eyes were bloodshot from liquor and exhaustion and fervor. "We bedded us plenty'a nigger sows in our younger days, you bet your bottom nickel on that. From Savannah to New Orleans we had ourselves some brief excesses and joyous bouts before the War of Northern Aggression started and the country went all to hell. Shared a few of those same women, too, that's the truth. You never know rightly, boy, maybe it's me who's your daddy. I bet I slept with your ole black mama more times than Septemus, and he done the deed plenty."

Priest knew the reasons for his own hatred and rage, but he wasn't quite sure why the hell everybody else was always so cantankerous, especially the rich and prosperous.

Chuckling with a killer edge, Lamarr said, "Don't suppose you're a staunch supporter of the viewpoints of Mr. Frederick Douglass."

"Can't say that I am. You know, I used to bring in renegade bucks like you for a pretty dollar."

That got Lamarr's attention. Both he and Priest sat up a little straighter, sharpened their focus. So Jowett was a former slave-catcher. Proud of the fact and stupid enough to puff his chest out about it. Priest was pretty sure they didn't need Jowett along on this raid in the first place, but he still didn't want to see things go lethal less than five minutes after the man walked in.

Lamarr said, "Well, now."

"I recollect your name. I remember you running in the Ohio Valley, that so?"

"Sure is."

After Lamarr had killed the slave master, he'd made a run up to northeast Ohio aided by sympathetic farmers, a fugitive on the Underground Railroad before he finally joined the Union Army. The slave-catchers hunted him state to state across the Midwest while he hid out in stations from Kentucky to the Pennsylvania border. He was stowed along with cargo, stuffed in the bottom of false-bottom wagons by Railroad agents they called conductors.

The ultimate goal was to get to "Heaven," which was the slave code word for Canada. More than one abolitionist caught a beating and much worse for him, and the fact weighed heavily on Lamarr, even now.

"You ever make it to your Northern paradise, boy?"

"Not quite, but that's all right, I got close enough. I hid in caskets, packed four deep with the dead. I didn't need to live in them there Canadian wilds. Just about anyplace was heaven compared to Georgia."

Now Priest understood a little more about why Lamarr had laid himself out in the coffins, and how he could fall asleep so easily in them.

"Too bad we never met back then," Jowett said, " 'neath the stars. Coulda shared us a pint or two 'fore I brought you home again."

"Wouldn't'a claimed much for me, I expect. I was poor property."

"So they woulda just tied you to the lynchin' tree."

"I suspect."

Talk about the cotton fields was about the only thing that managed to get a barb through Lamarr's skin, but he was taking it admirably so far. Of course, having your finger on a trigger went a long way to satisfying a man. But the tension kept growing, tightening another knot in the noose.

Lamarr said, "Mr. Douglass contended that killin' a slave hunter was as proper as the slaughter of a ravenous wolf."

"That right?"

"It is. Not that I got anything 'gainst wolves, mind you."

"If Douglass and I'd ever run across each other we would've had us a discussion about that subject he wouldn't have liked a'tall. And now them Yankee bastards got more worries on their hands than they ever expected, with uppity niggers runnin' hog wild in their streets."

"Think they're sorry Sherman left Atlanta in flames?"

148

"Some of them, I'd wager, regret the part they played in the war."

"Don't suppose you recall Appomattox fondly much, now do you?"

"No, I do not."

"We all got our reasons to mourn."

Priest knew just enough about the Fugitive Slave Act of 1850 to understand how deadly the moment had become. Lamarr almost couldn't force his smile any longer, and that was something Priest had never seen before. Jowett seemed to think he could still turn Lamarr in somewhere down on the Chattahoochee River and collect a bounty. For some folks, the Civil War hadn't ended and never would. There were still two countries going for each other's throats.

The federal ordinance, meant to appease Southern states threatening to secede from the Union, gave wide authority to slave-catchers and forced local law enforcement officials to help them. Lamarr had gone up against plenty of sheriffs and bounty hunters in his time, making his run for Canada. According to Lamarr, the ordinance only angered most Northerners even more, and the ranks of those willing to assist runaways swelled with merciful folk.

Some of Lamarr's songs weren't his

mother's, but a language runaways used to alert one another. Priest had to imagine Lamarr's booming voice cut down to a whisper, murmuring that a fierce wind was blowing in from the South, which meant a slave hunter was in town. It was almost impossible to think of Lamarr as ever being afraid of anything.

Jowett's gaze settled squarely on Priest for the first time. "You're McClaren."

"Yep."

"Heard about you some, too. Heard that your baby sister is the real man of the family."

"You do come by an awful lot of information."

"It pays for a man to know as much as he can."

"Especially an ignorant fraud like you."

That brought Jowett's head up as if he'd been rapped on the chin. "We had to tar and feather plenty of nigger lovers, too."

"You people sure kept yourselves amused."

"That we did. Might have to do some more so I stay diverted."

Priest tried to give back one of Lamarr's broad smiles, but it just didn't work for him. "You're welcome to try."

"No telling what could happen 'fore this is all over."

"Sure."

Jowett finished his whiskey, drew his boots back on, and asked, "There a good, clean brothel in this town?"

"No," Priest said. The thought of this short bastard's hands on one of Patty's girls, those stumpy legs kicking up the sheets, turned Priest's stomach.

"Goddamn Septemus for dragging me into these ungodly parts of the country. If that son of a bitch is still alive I might just stretch his neck a few inches myself." There were the remains of a crisp unease. "I'll be staying at his ranch. I'll be in touch in the next day or so to let you know how this will go. Either of you don't follow my orders to the letter, I'll leave you in Mexico to die."

That didn't quite sound like Sarah's promise that Hatcher Jowett would help in whatever capacity was needed.

Jowett stood and stepped out the door without closing it behind him, got on his horse, and rode toward town.

The wind rose and thumped against the shack walls, prying at the corners of the roof. Crimson and purple streaks of dawn striped the ridges and hills. The air was chilled and pervaded with mesquite.

Lamarr looked over at Priest and told him, "I'm starting to get the feelin' this

151

might not be the most pleasurable trip I ever had down Mexico way."

"I've known your hunches to be wrong before," Priest said, "but I believe this one's dead on the nail."

"Those sure were some ugly pants on that son of a bitch, wasn't they?"

Chapter Eight

Folks walked out of Freerson's Dry Goods Emporium carrying barrels of salt pork and jerky, sacks of oats and barley, jars of syrup, and other provisions. Down the road, buckboards bustled by. Men yelled amiably behind the livery sheds, and the children played mumblety-peg down on Broad Street, leaping into mud puddles to the screeches of their mothers.

Cowpunchers and farmers, bound for the saloon, met at the hitching post and discussed the best places to eat in town. Tobacco smoke hung in a thick smog around their mouths before swirling off in the breeze.

An owl skimmed close to the ground. Shadows loomed between the buildings, and Priest wondered if Gramps might be hiding somewhere out there, in transition, or if he was already on the mountain.

Molly was cooking some kind of food Priest had never seen before. The pan bubbled and spewed bits of vegetables and meat he didn't recognize, surrounded by simmering dirty rice. She'd learned all kinds of tricks on the trail, ways to prepare weeds and roots and other things he didn't want to think about. He'd eaten worse, he figured, though he couldn't exactly remember when.

Right now she was chopping hell out of peppers and the gray flank of an animal she must've caught herself in the hills. It was a good turn of luck that he'd already told her he wasn't hungry.

Wooden wind chimes rang out a doleful melody. She'd taken to hanging them around the porch just as their grandmother had. Priest had pulled a rocking chair into the dining room and sat holding the baby, slowly creaking back and forth the way Pa used to do on Sunday afternoons before breaking out his fiddle.

It was all right to be swept away by the past on days like this. Katie cooed in Priest's arms and he drew her up a little tighter, hoping the *Ga'ns* spirits weren't peering at the baby over his shoulder, trying to get in.

A jug full of fresh-cut wildflowers sat in

the center of the table. Priest hadn't been sure his sister could settle back down in Patience after the life she'd led but she'd taken to it well enough, this cleaning and cooking and caring for the baby.

"Braulio," she said, and the name hung between them. She glanced over at him, set her lips, shook her head, and gave him that "you've been a bad boy" scowl. "When I said if you ever needed help you could come to me, I didn't expect you to take me up on it so soon."

"Neither did I. So you 'ran across' him, too?"

"Yep."

"Jesus. There any trouble you didn't find yourself neck-deep in at one time or another?"

"Not much. You can put her down in the crib if you want."

Katie started for his eyebrows again and he had to rear his head back to keep them where they belonged. "That's all right, I like holding her. But this Braulio . . . what can you tell me about him?"

She tossed the gray meat onto the grill, where it hissed, sounding alive and angry. "That you don't want to make a run against him. Especially not for that bastard Septemus Hart. Braulio's a desperado who enjoys the lifestyle and power it gives him. All that stolen money hasn't made him fat and lazy the way it does most of them. You want to stay clear."

Priest nodded, pursed his lips, and remained silent.

"Are you listening to me? You got no reason in the world to put yourself on that line."

"Lamarr would go without me. I can't let him do that."

Her singed cheekbones caught the light and appeared like two angry wounds cut into her face. "That brings me to something else I've been intending to mention."

"Okay."

"The both of you aren't so good for each other as I might have once thought."

"What do you mean?"

"You both got similar weaknesses in your character."

"We do?" He'd never dwelled on that.

Turning the steaks over but letting them cook too long, Molly watched them sizzle. "It drives you to do the same stupid things."

"My, ain't you just a room full of sunshine."

"No," she admitted, "I'm not, and don't ever expect me to be. I'm your sister and I want to look out for you."

She didn't realize how much that twisted him up, hearing advice—and good advice at that—from his teenage sister, who was more levelheaded than he ever would be. Jowett's words about Molly being the man of the family came back again, and Priest felt the muscles of his back tighten, the heat crawling up his spine.

"A friend should be busy talking you out of these ticklish ventures," Molly said, "not into them."

"Truth of the matter is that I'm the one who told him."

"One or the other, it don't make much of a difference. That's my point. You pull each other into trouble."

"So far—"

"Yeah, I know, so far you've done all right pulling each other through, too. But how long you think that's gonna last, Priest?"

It made him grin, knowing that she cared about him this much. Molly saw the smile and frowned, those full pink lips coming out to pout now. He wanted to explain it to her, tell her the same thing he'd told Patty. That your loved ones were as good as blood, whoever they were, for whatever reason, and that the rest would sort itself out or it wouldn't.

But Molly had been on her own for so

long, relying on only herself, that she didn't understand how most folks couldn't make it on their lonesome. He studied her for a moment, once again impressed by her knowledge and strength, all that sly skill and subtle capability. How had she managed it?

"Put the baby down, it's time to eat."

Priest carried Katie to her crib, laid her on her belly beside one of the corn husk dollies that Lamarr had made her. A shamefully ugly thing with blind button eyes that gazed through clots of yellow yarn. He rubbed the infant's back, reached and drew his fingers through her fuzzy hair. His resolve solidified, renewed.

Molly had set three places and started spooning the stew out into the plates.

"Gramps back?" he asked hopefully.

"Sometimes he comes in during the night, steals a little food, and vanishes again."

"Oh, Christ."

"He doesn't always run right to the Apaches. On occasion he skulks around town for a day or two, hiding in the alleys. I use a lot of spices, same as Mama did. The smell might bring him around."

"Your way of making sure he's fed."

"I do what I can."

She ate fast, like it might cost her dearly to be caught holding a spoon. Her trail instincts might never give out completely. Molly eating quick as she could, on the lookout, on the prod. Her golden curls flapped about as she chewed heartily, cool blue eyes on him, considering, trying to understand.

The food was much better than he'd expected, and he finished everything on his plate. She fed him seconds and he ate that as well.

"Guess I was more hungry than I reckoned," he told her.

"It happens like that," she said. "Used to be that when I was nervous about something, or excited, I wouldn't want so much as a bite. The thought of grub would make me nauseous. I'd start gagging. But if I did take that first bite, even if it was only a spoonful of beans, I'd suddenly be famished and would load up like I'd been starved for weeks."

Priest stared down at his empty plate, still hungry, and couldn't decide if he was mostly nervous or excited, too. "You were going to tell me about Braulio."

She rubbed her fingers together, the missing tips of her pinkies and top knuckle of her left ring finger having been

159

lost to frostbite. Her earlobes were gone too, but her lengthening hair now hid the fact. She clenched and unclenched her small fists the way you might expect a sheriff or bounty hunter to do preparing for a gunfight. Except she hadn't done any of that when she'd beaten Septemus's gunny Griff to the draw and shot him in the teeth.

Molly took his hand and walked with him to the sitting room and they both took seats facing one another again, the silence growing peaked, getting a bit sharp.

"You can't do it, Priest. Not for Hart. And not because of that Sarah. She's only toying with you, that much is clear as the ears on a mule. Tossed you out of her life, cleaved unto him, and the minute things go to hellfire she calls you back to suffer in his stead."

She was probably right, but he didn't want to hear it again. These same sentiments had been running loose in his head for three days. "I've made up my own foolish mind, Molly. Just another stupid thing I'm driven to do."

"You're a damn idiot."

"Help me to plan it, if you can."

With a pained huff she relented. The emotion in her voice brought out the childlike, singsong quality even more prominently. "I've heard of that pueblo. I got near it one time about eighteen months ago but never had need to get too close. I trailed a woman-killer name'a Willie Landay down that way. By the time I caught up to him he was dead."

"Braulio did the killing? With a throwing blade?"

"You know about him and his knives? What he does with them?"

Nodding, holding her gaze, Priest said, "Padre Villejo told us." He withdrew the perfectly balanced knife, held it out to her.

"That one of his?"

"Yep."

"It's evil. Throw it down a mine shaft and don't look back."

"Not just yet."

"Why? You want to kill him with his own blade? Don't do that to yourself. There's Indian tribes that believe if you steal a man's weapon and murder him with it, you're damned to carry his soul on your back the rest of your life."

Someone else would've called that only a superstition she'd picked up one place or another on the trail. He wouldn't.

"Did Braulio stab this Landay you were after?"

That focused Molly again. "No. Willie took what he wanted from any woman he came

161

across. Mexes, Apaches, whites, old, young, didn't matter to him. If they resisted he had this derringer he'd put to their foreheads. Hardly any gunpowder in his shot at all. Charge was so weak that sometimes the bullet didn't even break the skin, but it was usually enough to crack their skulls. And that ain't the worst of it."

He didn't want to hear the worst of it, but there wasn't much choice.

"There's ladies out there still alive that can't do much but slobber and moan like an animal 'cause'a what he did to them."

"Jesus."

Sometimes he could almost forget the trials his sister had gone through in her years crossing the country looking for Yuma Dean, and then the guilt would swell in him, like now, until he couldn't meet her eyes.

"Willie was worth twice as much alive as he was dead, but I didn't mind losing a few hundred dollars in that particular case."

"No, I suppose you wouldn't. How do we get to the pueblo?"

"You won't have to go too far. Eighty-five, ninety miles south of the river. Not much local water that way, either. A goat herder's tank about ten miles east of there. His spread is on a green plateau that's little more than an oasis surrounded by wasteland. He's holed up in the middle of hell. What you need to watch for are the defenses. Two rings of guards, three miles out on the cliffs, and another group closer to the village. Regular posts along the high ridges. Scouts out between the canyons, at the crossings."

"He's got that many men?"

"A lot more now, I'd guess, than a year and a half ago. Most of these bandit outfits don't last long 'cause they're always on the run from the law, hiding in the hills, stealing from each other and fighting among themselves. They're lazy and when they start going hungry they cut their strings and scurry off. But Braulio's stayed sharp. The people come to him, in droves, and he cares for those under his protection. It's been a very bad couple of years down there."

"So it's all ego? Like with Septemus?"

"I think so. Braulio doesn't want to retire rich, he only wants money 'cause it gives him a long reach over a lot of people. He's got enough gold to provide him pull with the armies on both sides of the border, enough women and liquor to keep the men happy. The Mex government would rather get paid off than fight skirmishes with him for the next five or ten years."

"How close did you get to his camp?"

"Not very. Willie slipped past the first ring of guards and I followed him. Two or three men on the canyon walls before the land breaks into the plateau. He didn't hold his own against the second perimeter. That's another several men set about a mile outside the town who patrol the area. They had some fun with him before they strung him up to bleed out. Shot him pretty much to pieces, but they took their time. The stories, Priest. They say nobody dies quick by Braulio's hand. It takes hours. Sometimes days."

Priest drifted, seeing yellowed lacy tatters of Donna Angelina Allasandro's dusty wedding gown, trying to puzzle it all out. What he should be feeling, and how the layout of strategy should go. It wasn't his strong suit. In the end his heavy thoughts only made him sleepy, and he wanted to ride the drowsiness down into darkness.

"Stay the night," she said. "I might be able to teach you a few things tomorrow that might help."

"Thanks."

"Gramps won't be back, so you can bunk in his bed. But if you hear any snarling and rattling around in the kitchen after the moon's up, it ain't a wildcat, it'll be him."

* * *

164

In the morning, he found her readying the horses, the saddlebags stuffed with clinking glass. "We going somewhere?"

"Are you any good with a gun or rifle?"

"Not really," Priest said. "Maybe fair on a good day."

"Lamarr's one of the best shots in town. Hasn't he ever given you lessons?"

"No."

"You should ask."

"I did once. He couldn't really show me what he was doing or explain how he did it. For him, it comes so natural and he had no way to relate it to me."

Molly tied a black bandanna around her throat. "Like you and a knife."

"I suppose so."

"We'll head out to the hills. There's a spot there where I practice on bottles. I could give you a few instructions that might benefit you some."

"We'll be leaving for Mexico in the next few days. Think it'll help in such short order?"

"Won't make you worse anyways. I'll get Mrs. Wentworth from next door to watch Katie for a couple of hours."

They stepped inside, and she opened her trunk and drew out several weapons that had been carefully wrapped in oiled cloth. Molly extracted the guns, checked each one to make sure it wasn't loaded, spun the chamber, cocked the hammer close to her ear, and then slowly released it.

She said, "You never pull the trigger unless you're planning to kill somebody. You never point a pistol unless you're going to shoot. You never draw unless you intend to aim and fire. You understand?"

"Yes."

"You sure?"

"Yep."

She looked over at Priest, who had never been much at ease around pistols. He tried not to show how put off he was and she couldn't quite hold back a sad smile.

The slight click of the hammer easing back into place reminded Priest of sitting in the chair stained with his mother's blood and emptying Pa's Remington Frontier. 44 into Spider Rafe's corpse lying on the floor. All of Priest's nerves contracted into his left hand, just like that afternoon, and no matter how he tried he couldn't control the terrible trembling in his last two fingers.

"That still happens to you?" she asked.

"Only the second time since that day."

"You're edgy, seeing me do what I do."

"Yep, I think so," he said, massaging the offending fingers with his good hand. "Still throws me a bit is all. I have a hard time re-membering you're only seventeen, and that becoming a manhunter was your calling."

"Don't hold it against me, it's who I am."

"If anything, I take exception with my-self. I'm your older brother. I should've been the one to live the life you've led."

"That's a bold statement. And a pre-sumptuous one."

"How's that?"

"You make it sound as if I've had an un-happy last few years. They weren't. I had a grand old time from one day to the next, and I wouldn't trade any of it. I'm young, healthy, well-off, and have the most beauti-ful baby girl ever seen in this town. So you can stop feeling sorry for me. You had your own burden to carry, and when the time came you stood up just fine under the load."

She replaced several pistols before set-tling on a double-action .41 Colt Lightning revolver. The only reason he knew what kind of gun she held was because it was the same kind Burial Jones Clay had tried to blow the back of Lamarr's head off with. Molly's Colt had a rare set of one-piece grips, tiger-striped with delicate checker-ing and fireblue screwheads.

"This is a good gun for you. Colt is the

best. Don't let anybody sway you any differently."

Priest's fingers flapped even worse, and he tried to ball his hand into a fist and grind the fist against his leg, but still his pinkie stuck way out, twitching severely. "All right."

"Here, take this one. See if you're comfortable with it."

The second he touched that striped grip the tangled nerves in his hand were fine. "Feels good. Do you have two?"

"What do you need two for?"

"In case I lose one."

She wet her lips. "You pulling my leg?"

"No," he said, and she handed him another.

Next, she studied him, noting his height, the length of his arms. She hunted in the trunk for the right rifle for him. She settled on a Winchester .44-40. "Take the ammunition I got set aside there. Always save your shells when practicing. Squander them and you're wasting money."

"I understand."

He remembered her at twelve years old, practicing with Pa's Colt .45 pistol and the Remington Frontier .44. Priest had immediately taken to the bottle, enjoying his blackouts so much that he had only scraps and fragments of the months following their parents' murders. Once he'd woken up in the middle of a sentence and Molly had to prompt him to get him going again. He'd been showing her how to tie a bedroll and make camp. She had such clarity and resolve that his shame at being a drunk sent him running back to the whiskey every minute he was awake.

Gramps taught her everything she needed to know about the trail. The *Ga'ns* spirits were taking further hold of him by then as he was coasting out of his white life. He told her how to lay on coals in winter, find water in the desert, and live on the outskirts of an unfriendly town. He had a grunt in his voice, rehearsing to be an Apache.

It took only those six weeks for Molly to become submerged within the new kid, the woman bounty hunter she was on the verge of becoming. Darkly determined, adamant, with an unclouded vision and sense of direction as she began the pursuit of Yuma Dean. Sometimes he couldn't recall the little girl she'd once been, and it often felt like there had never been another Molly at all. By then she didn't look like a girl anymore, or even a boy, but instead appeared to be a raging short man that nobody would want to cross, some kind of afflicted dwarf.

She could still smile and laugh and talk the way she always did, but you just couldn't see a young girl there anymore, not even if you were looking the way he always did, not even if you knew one was supposed to be there. She wouldn't have any problems playing her role because it wasn't a role and never had been. She could drink whiskey in any bar and get a room in a hotel if she had the cash and even the sidewinders would steer clear for the most part. Her eyes were chips of shale, and Priest realized even in his drunken stupidity that although he wasn't afraid of his twelve-year-old sister, he should've been.

He had realized that she was going to get something done, and that he probably never would. It was only blind, hideous luck that allowed him to find Yuma Dean at Septemus's ranch and kill him.

"You're getting that look in your eye again," Molly said.

"What look?"

"The one that says you're wrapping the past up around you like a faded, ripped bed sheet."

"Yeah?"

"Keep your mind on the job, Priest. Braulio will, of that you can be damn certain."

170

"Let's go," he said.

They took the baby next door to Mrs. Wentworth, who proved to be a buxom woman of about thirty whose face lit up when she saw Katie. Two little boys, maybe four or five years old, came to the front door and held onto their mother's skirts, shy but enamored of Molly and trying to get her attention. Both of them kept saying her name, then giggling as they hid behind their mama, peeking out, red-faced. Mrs. Wentworth offered freshly baked pie and milk, but Molly declined in her courteous, amiable manner while Priest just nodded, tipped his hat.

Up in the hills, they practiced on rows of differently shaped tonic and patent-medicine bottles, some so small and transparent that Priest could barely see them.

Molly taught him that it didn't matter how fast you can fire a pistol, it's how quickly you can fire it accurately. First step was gun movement and quick drawing while maintaining sight alignment. Consistency was the key to accurate shooting, she kept telling him, and he wondered who had taught her.

Maintain a body position that affords you proper support for your weapon, she taught him. She drummed it into him that how you hold your rifle or pistol will directly affect how accurately you shoot. An even, unhindered grip works best.

More basics. Momentarily hold your breath, just before you take your final aim and pull the trigger, and make sure you remove that extra shaking you get from inhaling and exhaling. Take one or two full breaths and release the air as you squeeze off a shot.

"Jesus Christ," he said, "this is the way you and Lamarr do it?"

"Me, yes. Him, he was born knowing, I think. Go collect the shells and set up more bottles."

Priest did as he was told. His sister continued with the lessons, showing him the proper way to draw. Concentrate on a specific point, don't just aim at the target. Select a small location on the mark and aim at that spot. He kept trying for the bottles, hitting one out of every ten draws.

Molly kept up a steady stream of encouragement no matter how shitty he actually shot. She didn't let him drift, kept talking about Braulio and Willie Landay. Her voice took on a steady tone of solemn instruction. She'd done this before, possibly many times over.

"Your target and sighting post should be

aligned and in focus. Try looking away briefly and then looking back before taking final aim, that'll help you to center. Being consistent about your sight picture is really important. Whether you decide to shoot with one eye closed or both eyes open, be consistent; don't change midstream. Smooth and precise pull on the trigger."

"Okay."

"Shh, listen." She repeated herself knowing he couldn't get it all down the first time around. "When pulling the trigger, you use the tip of your finger and draw straight back. Don't lower the gun after each shot to check the hits. Keep your eyes focused as you recover from recoil."

"Goddamn thing," Priest said. "I'll never have a taste for it."

"Normally, I'd say that was good. Men who love guns hardly ever live to see gray in their beards. But against Braulio . . ."

"I know."

Molly spit and fired from the hip, showing off a little, firing three times in quick succession and smashing three green bottles. Shards flew in every direction, the three stoppers thumping into the dirt. She fired three more times, each of the stoppers exploding in turn.

173

"I think maybe I should go with you," she said.

He'd been expecting her to say that since he'd first asked her for help. He felt a small, instant sense of relief and then an abrupt searing guilt.

Where did you go when your baby sister shamed you by being more undaunted and braver than you were? He wanted to tell her of course not, it was foolish, she wasn't even eighteen yet, and this was man's work, except that she was better at it than he'd ever be.

"No, Molly," he said. "You've got a child to care for now. Besides, Lamarr's got a few fancy tricks that will help out. We'll make it all right."

"That Sarah's not worth it, Priest. Let her go after that stinking runt bastard if she loves him so much."

Priest just stared at her.

"It doesn't even bother you, really, me talkin' about her this way. You don't love her anymore, no matter what you might declare to yourself. You don't even know why you're doing this, do you? Risking your life, traveling into a place you got no reason to be. Do you?"

"Molly, listen—"

"Hell with that. You want to hear why? You've never been able to figure it out on your own these last few years. They're harsh words but they need to be said, so I'll say 'em." She moved in on him, got close the way Sarah did, arching her neck back to stare up into his face. "It's because you've got your heart set on pain."

Priest turned, took the proper stance, kept an even, unhindered grip, held his breath for an instant and selected a small location on the target and aimed at that spot, released his breath, pulled the trigger with the tip of his finger, did everything right.

He missed.

Chapter Nine

Sheriff Amos Burke sauntered over and took in the scene with a smirk, seeing Hatcher Jowett wearing those ugly pants, in his saddle while his horse nudged at Lamarr's, the two of them waiting out front of Molly's house as she held the whimpering baby on the porch and Priest holstered the Colt and got ready to go with them.

"My, my," Burke said, "I believe my invitation to this soiree must've been misplaced."

He put a little extra swagger into his walk now as he quickened his pace and moved across the street toward them. Call him what you like, he could sniff out impending trouble, especially when it concerned Lamarr and Priest. The morning light threw a glint against his badge and his bottom gold teeth, his spurs jangling out a small, unpleasant tune. He tried to keep his gaze nailed steadily to Priest but he couldn't help glancing around at the others, especially Jowett, who kept snapping his weighted quirt into his palm in a sign of growing impatience.

Children played hide-and-seek at the other end of the alley, and the old men in front of Freerson's Dry Goods Emporium chattered about whores they'd known back in the border camps. Burke stayed true to his preferred form and kept posing, showing off his profile first and then angling to the left side and then the right, the way he always did.

No one said anything until Molly broke the silence with, "Sheriff, nice to see you this morning."

"Likewise, Miss McClaren. I notice these horses are all packed up for traveling. You leaving us again, Molly?"

"No, it's not me this time."

"Well, then."

The quirt came down again and again in Jowett's hand, the repetitive noise designed to marshal attention to him without his ever having to say a word. Priest thought of the slaves that must've cowered at that sound as Jowett strolled the plantation, kicking across the cotton fields, agony drawing closer.

Jowett asked, "You Burke?"

You could see how the sheriff took offense to the tone and attitude of Hatcher Jowett, who sat astride his horse with his stumpy legs, leaning down a touch like he might throw himself into Burke's chest at any second. Priest thought it was nice to see two men he disliked having a dislike for each other.

"I am."

"Heard a lot about you from Septemus Hart."

"You're an acquaintance of Mr. Hart?"

"That's right, he and I go back to before the war, not that I'm disposed to tell you my business. He allows that you're a man who knows his duty and sense of obligation, much of the time."

Burke didn't know how to take that, so he grinned vaguely as if it might be a compliment. "That I do."

"I respect his discretion and insight into men's characters."

"My daddy do a fine job of judging men," Lamarr said. "That be the truth."

"I'd agree to that," Priest said.

"Figured you would, seeing as how my daddy estimated us to be the only ones who might come save his skinny ass in such a time of need."

"You suppose he considers us to be of

179

strong moral constitution or piss poor?"

Lamarr toyed with the strap of his sombrero, pondering the question. "Now that you mention it, I gotta admit that I ain't made up my mind on that yet."

"It does pose a perplexing riddle."

"That it does. In fact, I—"

"Would you two shut your damn mouths?" Jowett barked. "Or are you going to tempt my Christian sensibilities all the way to the border?"

"No, suh. Not with us, you won't have yourself no trouble. You and Daddy both got our respect, being men of perception and prudence."

"You sassing me again, boy?"

"Oh no, not me, suh."

Burke liked his trials plain and simple, and this one confused him. All the banter, the tension in the air without any direction. He was a lawman who didn't like mysteries or puzzles, and he couldn't see his way through any seriously tangled problem.

"I want to know what goes on here," he said.

Priest and Lamarr ignored him, started urging their horses forward while Burke hit another pose, throwing his chest out, trying to flaunt the badge.

"Now step away, son," Jowett said, turning aside with saddlebags packed with twenty thousand dollars, "we prefer not to lose any daylight."

Their trail took them through barren, broken country covered with little more than lizards and vermin. They passed a couple of depleted pueblos where the starving, half-naked people eyed them with fear and contempt. Barefoot women in dull skirts and serapes carried jugs on their heads, their thin hips swinging hurriedly. Three teenage girls were trying to shoe a bucking mule—staring openly, being friendly in a place like this. Fists held against her belly, their mother called them inside, harsh and grating: "Carmen, Teresa, Rocio, *vamos.*" They went, and the little mule shit and trotted off.

Lamarr hardly ever quit smiling except when he caught sight of the dark, vacant-eyed Mex children who didn't even bother to beg.

"These are called the years of sadness," Lamarr said.

Jowett lifted his chin. "Are there any other kind for a Mex?"

They passed through several dry washes cut from past flash floods, taking the slight sandy rises slowly before they crossed the river and headed on toward the desert.

Dust devils whirled across the empty

land. Priest had never been this far from home before and it gave him both an odd thrill and a flutter of dismay. Was Molly right? Had he come this way just to cause himself further pain in preparation for his dying?

They ate chili and leathery tortillas that were so chewy you could eat only one before your jaw got tired. During the nights, Lamarr and Priest took turns on watch for bandits and Federales, one of them always keeping an eye on Jowett as well. The man didn't mind, it just meant he got more sleep. He always bunked on the far side of the camp with his head on the stuffed saddlebags, his dreams propped up on twenty thousand dollars.

"I never seen that much money before," Lamarr said as the fire burned low and the stars lost themselves in the lightening ruby skies of dawn. Priest had been awake for about ten minutes and hadn't opened his eyes or stirred, but he wasn't at all surprised that Lamarr knew he was no longer sleeping. "You think if I asked real nice he let me take a peek?"

Priest sat up and glanced over. "I suspect he still might not allow it, no matter how sweet tempered and polite you might be."

"Most I ever seen was when a bank manager at the Bird Cage embezzled and absconded with eighty-three hundred dollars."

"A fair amount of cash to depart with." Then, thinking of Lorelei and the sounds she and her client made upstairs, he said, "Them bankers apparently do like to spend their off hours at cathouses. Let me guess. The lovely and limber Fatima got something to do with how this story ends?"

"In a manner of speaking. See, this banker, he hadn't exactly planned out his great scheme over a lengthy course of time. As I recall, he met Fatima on a Saturday night and that Monday afterward, just when five o'clock came about, he shooed his tellers and employees off, locked up his office, cleaned out the vault, and skipped right on over to the Bird Cage. Landed all that money at Fatima's feet and her other personables."

"How'd you see it?"

"I was near at hand, you might say."

"And being a good and lawful citizen, she immediately called in the marshal? Or am I wrong?"

Lamarr gave him a wounded look, cocked his head, and let out a pained sigh. "You make the baby Jesus cry, making such hurtful comments on Fatima's integrity and repute."

"I do apologize."

Lamarr smiled again. "All right then.

Anyhow, the glorious Fatima didn't rouse that marshal immediately, as you suggested, but she did call in the deputies later on that night after that banker went drifting off to sleep."

"She's a righteous woman in her own way."

"My point being—"

"I think I understand. You want to leave Septemus to his fate, grab the satchel, and toss that twenty thousand at Fatima's personables."

With his eyes wide, nodding a little now, Lamarr said, "Well, I admit I never even thought on that any, but now that you mention it, I like the idea just fine. But the original intention of my tale was this . . . the eighty-three hundred dollars took four stuffed saddle bags for that there banker to carry. The only reason he stole exactly that amount was because that's all this skinny banker man could carry."

Priest hadn't considered it before. What did twenty thousand in cash look like? He'd never seen even a tenth of that at any one time.

"You think Jowett kept the money for himself? Cached it someplace?"

Lamarr pursed his lips, gave Priest one of his true stares, the kind Priest hated to see. "Or maybe there never was any ransom to give."

"How do you mean?"

Lamarr chose his words cautiously, a mood settling between them. "You ever think that maybe Sarah ain't quite as in love with Septemus as you might think she is? That this kidnapping is a turn of good fortune for her, to have the man's money without having the man no more?"

It was the kind of notion that had struck Priest plenty of times these last few months, and he still wasn't sure where he stood on it. Is it any worse to have your love abandon you for another man than it is to have her leave you for that other man's wealth?

On the one hand, she was sincere and devoted, even if she was being true only to someone else. On the other, she wanted only material fortune.

"As much as I'd like to know," he said, "I'm blind to the answer. Sarah isn't the kind of woman who cares about money above all else. But—"

"Yeah?"

"I never thought she'd leave me for that short old Reb bastard in the first place."

"Well, then."

No, Priest thought, she should've gone to

185

someone who could give her a child. That's what had driven them apart, the sorrow of the miscarriage.

If only—if only somehow she'd carried the child to full term . . . what then? Would they still be together, a happy, meaningful family? If you weren't already crazy, then you could make yourself such.

Yawning, crawling from his blankets, Hatcher Jowett ran a hand through his thinning hair and scratched at his neck. His gaze focused, and he spit into the dead fire. "Neither of you sons'a bitches boiled any coffee yet?"

The next day, beyond the river, they passed a shallow, slow-moving stream and spotted several gray and blue peaks rising in the distance, a stark range of shadow. The horses stretched their necks, dipped their muzzles in the water, and snorted lightly. All around was nothing but hummocks of small gnarled greasewood and clusters of cholla cactus. They passed through more empty towns and abandoned rancheros that had already been looted.

The morning broke hot and there was nothing to see but the heat-shimmering land and low brush. Priest could feel the straining inside himself, the doubts growing as he tried to lose himself within his purpose, even if he believed in it less now than before. He kept an ear out for the child, hoping to hear some good advice, but there was nothing.

About an hour after sunup Jowett found a tarantula in his vest pocket.

He squealed and slid backward off his horse, dancing in tiny circles, trying to smack the huge spider from his chest. He flapped his shirt hoping to knock it free, but the tarantula held on. Jowett kept prancing and capering, and Lamarr let out all his booming laughter, pulled off his sombrero, and smacked his thigh with it.

Finally, Jowett found himself again, got up his nerve, and plucked the huge spider from over his heart. He held on to it an extra second as if asserting his will on the world, proving that he could keep it from biting him, then threw the critter down and ground it under his boot heel.

"That one?" Lamarr said. "I named her Dorrie last night, 'fore I put her in your clothes."

"You did this, you bastard?"

"Seemed like the kind'a woman you might be taken with. Dark and all lovey-crawly like a good woman should be. It's something you'd know about, seeing as how you bedded plenty'a nigger sows in your younger days. I'm sure you met you some women like Dorrie before. I'd bet my bottom nickel on that." He chuckled, letting it out like a growl. "Just a childish trick to be playin', I know, suh, but I figured you'd be considerable forgiving seeing as how you slept with my ole black mama more times than Septemus, and I hear tell he done the deed plenty."

Jowett let the tension slide from him, attempting to gather up some of his lost youth and slickness. It had been a long time since he'd run into somebody like Lamarr, and you could see how he was starting to get back into the game a bit, finding his resignation again. Priest could just imagine him and Septemus forty years ago, running around the plantations with their quirts and whips and bottles of whiskey, short lords of their humid and lush domains.

"I just might have to kill you 'fore this journey's over."

"You said something similar a few days back, but so far you ain't reached for that hog leg'a yours."

Priest thought this play had brought out something sanguine and assured in the man, maybe the dancing made him feel like he was in his prime once more. Jowett climbed back into his saddle, lit a cheroot, leaned over, and said, "I'm not in any rush, and appears clear to me that you aren't either. You might hide in coffins four corpses deep and trifle with spiders, but so far you've held back on your string."

"Oh, I got nothin' against a man trying to earn himself a fair wage. Even a slave-catcher got a right to feed his big fat mama."

"Or could be you love old Septemus and anticipate him wrapping his arms around your barrel chest and giving you a big ole kiss on your shiny forehead for all you done to save his ass."

"Hmmm," Lamarr said.

"Hoping he'll welcome you into his home after all these years, let you stroll across the property shouting orders to his men, introducing you to kings and politicians as his only son. That it? Bringing your mama up from Georgia and treating her like one of them African princesses you people talk about. Dress her up in silk and gold." He let loose with a quiet, rough laugh that eased from the corners of his mouth. "That what you're expecting, boy?"

Nobody else might be able to tell, but Jowett had gotten to Lamarr. The smile not quite as wide now, his eyes a touch more stony. "Sure, same as anybody would, and that there's a fact. Now come on, suh. Kiss your Dorrie good-bye and let's get on with this holiday."

Priest stared at Hatcher Jowett and tried to get beyond the severity, baseness, and churlish nature in order to view the enterprising, resourceful man he'd once been. A gentleman of means, refinement, and sophistication.

So much apparent ugliness to him, from one viewpoint, but there had to be something else in this type of grand aristocrat that would draw Sarah to a man just like him. Priest couldn't bring himself to believe she cared only about money.

He searched Jowett's eyes, seeking nobility, maybe dignity, or simply a different kind of destructiveness that was worth forgiving in the end.

Jowett glowered. "And just what the hell, I ask, are you looking at?"

Priest said nothing. The child had begun to whisper, but the words weren't clear. Maybe they'd come and maybe they wouldn't, but for now it was enough to know he was being spoken to again, and that he was keen on listening.

They came upon an empty goat herder's water tank and Priest said, "About ten miles of here."

"How you know that?" Jowett asked.

"My sister told me."

"She crossed tracks with this Braulio?"

"In a manner of speaking. She chased a wanted man down this way."

For a second it could've gone either way, Jowett weighing his odds and options, undecided on what kind of a man Priest might be.

"She must be a hell of a woman."

"She is."

"And young, too."

"Not even eighteen."

"With a child."

"Yep."

"Got quite a reputation for bringing in some truly callous lawbreakers. And putting more than a handful to rest."

Priest could feel Jowett pulling together threads, seeking a way to put whatever he learned to use, find a weakness, a means to deceive. He'd said it the other day. How it pays for a man to know as much as he can.

Glancing over, Priest noticed that Lamarr was watching him, an eyebrow cocked, sort of telling him to take a turn with the old man, see how difficult it was to deal with him. But Priest tried to let it ride, figuring they had enough on their minds already, troubles that had haunted them for so long they'd become like family.

"We'll be coming up on the first ring of defenses soon. There will be scouts on the canyon cliffs before the land breaks into a plateau. Molly said it's an oasis in the middle of a wasteland."

"Is she a good mother?" Jowett asked.

"What?"

"Your sister. Is she a good mother to her child?"

"Yes, she is."

"That counts for a great deal, especially in these days when our society and culture are in upheaval and discord." The strong Southern accent gave his words an extra tinge of consequence they didn't necessarily deserve. What Priest would've given to be able to talk like that.

"I suspect it's a might better than during the war."

"Certainly in some ways, that's truth. But it's also undeniable that, for the worse, this is the age of digression and meandering and aimlessness. Not as much money or grandness or personal history for us to impart upon our youth. Was a time you could count on your neighbor to stand watch at your back, to share his bread, to keep vigil over your children if a man wasn't able."

Priest was still waiting for him to get around to saying how any of this related to Molly and Katie. It took him a few more seconds to realize it was part of the game, twining you along into conversation that already had its destination, though you couldn't see it. Where was Jowett bringing him?

"I'd be a'feared to raise a son in these current provinces and unsettled times. It's hard going, with all the troubles we still haven't ironed away, the Union being what it is. But Septemus's wife, that lovely girl Sarah, she's a handsome, strong woman, could see that right off. Had a setback and a hard go-around after losing her baby before the poor thing could see the beautiful light of the world."

Christ, he'd even found out about the child.

So, that's how it was going to be. Priest figured he must be holding the knife, perhaps both his own blade and Braulio's as well, one in each hand, and knew it was true when the reins flapped against his roan's neck unattended. Did you kill a man just for mentioning the worst hurt you've ever suffered? Or did you hold on against your own evil? Jowett kept staring ahead without expression.

They didn't need him. They'd never needed him on this run, so why was he really here?

Lamarr had taken off his sombrero, wiped the band clean of sweat with his cuff, put it back on. Telling Priest in his own fashion, *Come on now, stab him and let's take the money, go buy Fatima and her friends some new shoes.*

But that Southern voice, so full of affectation and ceremony, coiled inside Priest's chest.

"Fortunately though, ole Septemus managed to do his husband's duty, which is only right. Old fart like him takes a young wife, he'd better do all he can to keep her satisfied and well appeased so she don't fall into another man's arms."

"Listen—," Priest said, sensing what was about to come, and realizing that Molly had been right, he did want pain, but only up to a point.

"Love will hold her for a while. Money might keep her happy for a time. But the only way to make sure she stays put is for a man to give her a baby. That's about all any woman wants, far as I can see. She hasn't completed her task in this world if she hasn't braved and endured the full experience of motherhood."

Now, having fine-tuned the moment about as much as he could, but still looking for an extra ounce of attention, Jowett struck a match, relit his cheroot, took three long puffs, and blew the smoke out low so it rose around the face of Priest's horse, the roan snorting and cutting channels through the haze.

Jowett snickered before saying, "So, if he isn't dead yet, make sure you congratulate him on the imminent arrival of his first child born in wedlock."

There it was.

Lamarr let out a sorrowful grunt, turned and opened his mouth, but Jowett cut him off. "Oh, that's right, boy, you aren't the only claim to Hart blood in these parts anymore. You can spend your time looking forward to seeing some blue-eyed, lily-skinned lad growing up on that ranch, heir to all that land, cattle, fortune, and city properties. Maybe he'll hire you to work his fields, seeing as how you've some experience in that area."

Feeling himself grinning without completely understanding why, Priest said, "Thanks for letting me know."

Jowett stared, a little annoyed at how easily Priest had taken the news. But Priest had gotten one answer about Sarah that he'd wanted. She loved Septemus, and yes, it was better to lose her to another man than to discover she cared only about assets and fortune.

The child continued to whisper. There was an understanding that went beyond the usual frustration and matters of men. The child had no one else now but Priest, and that was just fine, all things considered.

They wound around shelves cut from solid rock, scraping the twisting, rising sides of the crowded cliff slopes. Burros in pack trains leading down from the ancient dead mines had left carved prints an inch deep in the stone.

"Now this I can grow accustomed to," Jowett said. "Reminds me of the bluffs overlooking the Yazoo River back home."

"Ah, Vicksburg," Lamarr said. "A hell of a six-week siege it was when General Grant led the Union Army against the Reb stronghold on the Mississippi."

"You weren't there."

"A burning July that was, you'll remember. He once said to me, 'Lamarr, my trusted friend—'"

"They didn't allow nigger troops to see battle in sixty-three, though I would've enjoyed killin' a few more in my day."

"Quite right, no niggers allowed. So there we were, Uly and me, looking down from Champion's Hill, and he put his arm around me and said, 'Lamarr, my trusted friend, let's play cards—'"

"Grant never said that."

"Of course he did, I'd never lie about Uly. 'Lamarr, my trusted friend, let's play cards while we wait for them gray coats to cry for their mammies' soft titties.' And so we did, and my amigo Uly's the one who taught me to play faro, that day, the beginning of the siege."

Priest expected it was quite possibly true, and suddenly found himself with some bad feelings aimed at the former President Ulysses S. Grant. "Don't suppose you won many hands off the general, now did you?"

"Well, he did have experience on his side, but I had plenty of time during them weeks to catch up some. By that Fourth of July I had a few of his dollars in my pocket."

"Isn't that about when you joined up with Hooker?"

Lamarr let out a hoot and a roar of laughter just thinking about it again. "Indeed it was. He was a poor soldier, was Joseph Hooker, but the ladies would follow wherever his troops went. Spent some time on Lookout Mountain and Chattanooga."

But Jowett had fallen into a mood, thinking about the siege of Vicksburg, and wasn't about to let it go. Odd how a man could easily prod another but couldn't stand to be nudged in return. Priest was struck by the notion that they really weren't anything but a bunch of school-boys causing a ruckus.

Jowett barely opened his mouth when he spoke, and his gentlemanly Southern accent was obliterated by his ferocious memories. "They tried taking us with their navy and we turned them back but good. In June of sixty-two, Farragut came in below the city with two frigates and six gunboats, attempted to run the river fortifications, but we stopped him. At the end of that year, Grant was shut in Holly Springs and Sherman got lost in the swamps. Our commander General John Clifford Pemberton drove him even farther back, bless his hide!"

Nodding, Lamarr drew the back of his hand across his sweaty forehead. He looked over at Priest, who had never been to a war outside his own making, and spoke casually. "Things were about to change then, 'cause Uly didn't retreat none. Sherman wanted us to hide out in Memphis, but me and the general, we ran around to Louisiana and marched some and floated some for thirty miles south 'til we recrossed the river. It was a glorious, beautiful thing."

"Stupid as hell, you mean," Jowett seethed, "cutting his own supply lines. You all should have starved."

"Nah, we lived on righteousness and

pure thoughts, so it worked out just fine for the Union. We took Champion's Hill that May, and played us a lot of cards and did a good deal of fishin', too. Thought the Rebs might hold out more than six weeks, but I guess you all missed your mamas' biscuits and gravy too much."

Sometimes you could almost miss not having been a part of the blood and destruction because everybody you ran into had been. It tied them together and rooted them in history, no matter which side they'd fought for. They had their stories, convictions, and the distinction of having survived encounters that had taken hundreds of thousands of others.

Even now Priest knew that Lamarr and Jowett were finding common ground, having been in the same place at the same time. Thinking back to the battle, the smell of death on the Mississippi, the respect and fear of one another in the middle of strife and combat. If a veteran didn't have a friend nearby to discuss the war with, then an enemy would do.

It was that much a part of who they'd become. He didn't think any soldiers would ever admit to it, but to his mind there was a kind of esteem and maybe affection for their foes, long after all the killing.

They settled into a heavy silence for another half mile until the precipice and mountain ridges rose into sheer walls and escarpments. They dismounted and walked another hundred yards, yanking their horses behind them. Downdrafts brought in colder winds from the peaks.

"You see the lookouts?" Priest asked.

"Not yet," Lamarr told him, "but if I was a gambling man—"

"Which isn't to say you are."

"That's true, but if I was, I'd guess they were holed up behind those two outcroppings, the one right there"—his dark, scarred hand raised, gleaming and pointing—"and the other . . . way over there. Looks like a couple of trails leading into the canyon. Mountain snow runoff comes down that way, so they'll have fresh water."

"Molly said Willie Landay slipped past the first defense but got caught up by the second."

Shaking his head, Jowett swung halfway around and let his coat come swirling after him. It was a move that must've been impressive on the ballroom floors of Savannah. A dust devil surged at his ankle and dissipated. "This Willie Landay probably only thought he'd glided by the sentries here. No reason for them to deal with him if he was coming ahead anyway. One kept watch. The other ran back, alerted the next group, and they all took him down together."

"And strung him up and shot him to pieces." There were men who loved to torture and murder without much justification, but even most of them made a game of it, had a reason in the end. Whether they were after riches, revenge, or just to prove their strength and authority over others. But to string somebody up and shoot him to shreds? "Why? Where's the payoff in that?"

"Maybe to lure Molly out," Lamarr said, and his voice had an edge to it. Like he wished he'd been there to see such goings-on. "Maybe they thought she'd be stupid enough to come after them, try to save ole Willie."

"Yeah," Priest said, because it made sense. They wanted his sister. There was a reason, in the end. They wanted the girl. "But she outfoxed 'em."

"These *banditos* got all the money they need. Too much tequila, too many pretty *muchachas*. More than that, they're outlaws with enough pull to keep the Federales off their backs. That leads to mischief. The padre said this Braulio sang an old tune. Sounds about right to me."

"If they got all the money they need,

what do they want with twenty thousand more?"

"Now that there is a question we aimin' to answer."

So many things you never thought of before when you should've done so.

Jowett said, "We've been sworn safe passage, but it wasn't any gentleman who laid that claim. We're best off drawing those watchmen out and taking them down at ground level." He let loose with that quiet, rough laugh again, and it hung around his chin like cheroot smoke. "Only way to do that, as I see it, is to tickle their noses with the sweet perfume of plunder. They won't want to share with their cohorts. They'll want to dispose of us and take it for themselves."

"Sweet perfume of plunder?" Priest was sort of struck by the sound of the words. "I reckon they'll enjoy that, all right."

"Depends on how scared they are of Braulio," Lamarr said. "Which is bound to be plenty."

"Good thing we got an abundance of nectar to tempt them with." Jowett untied his saddlebags. "They'll want to make it easy on themselves, come down out of the rocks and use their rifles from the lowest ledge shelf. There."

"Uh-huh," Lamarr said. "They get enough

cash for themselves, they can run out on Braulio, stake a new territory."

"Be dark in an hour. We'll camp here. Start a fire so they can see us. There's going to be a lot of moon tonight. While they're climbing down, you two meet them on the shelf. If they're smart, they won't try anything until the moon begins to set. Keep one of 'em alive." Commanding others came naturally to Jowett, his shoulders back like he was going to wait on a salute. "Make him tell you exactly where the next set of lookouts are posted. We'll head up to the plateau at dawn and travel right through that second line of defense while the men are sleeping. They won't expect anything without the sentries raising an alarm. We're still a few days from the deadline."

Lamarr scratched at his red sash, took out his lasso, and started loosening the knot. "Funny how you still giving orders like you're in the army. You must've been an officer. Only an officer is so free with other men's lives."

"It was my honor to serve in the Confederacy Army as a captain. Same as Septemus."

"Okay, Cap'n. But it'll be me and you who wait on that shelf. Just like we lingered together for over forty days at Vicksburg."

"I told you how it was going to be done,"

Jowett said. He gave his little swing-around movement again, the coat swirling and snapping.

"Yes, suh, you did. But we're doin' it the way I said. Now, Cap'n, you just follow me."

Priest was surprised to hear Lamarr playing with the plans, but then realized Lamarr was only trying to protect him.

After they got the information from the lookouts, they'd have to kill the unarmed men, and Lamarr figured that he and Jowett—the two soldiers—already had enough blood on their hands that it wouldn't make much difference. Priest started to say something but hesitated. There should be another way to go about it, and if so, he should be able to see it clearly, and yet nothing was coming to him.

He found himself trying to imagine what Molly would do, and understood with a chill, as the downdraft swept the taste of snow to him, that she would've done the same thing.

Chapter Ten

The edges of night folded in around Priest as he stared into the fire. The icy stone of the canyon chewed through the blanket beneath him. He hoped Lamarr wouldn't take any chances with Jowett—despite the bonding of soldiers, the former slave-catcher would probably just as soon take Lamarr down as Braulio's men or anybody else.

Priest shifted the saddlebags beneath his head. He'd opened them and looked inside, seeing the wads of currency. Hundred-dollar bills that looked hastily bound together. He didn't count it all but figured it came to about twenty thousand. The money was old and had to be from Septemus's private stash, hidden away in a wall safe someplace on the hacienda. Purse change.

The sweet perfume of plunder. It stank of Septemus Hart and everything he stood for—of Priest's lost love, whiskey, and somehow even the blood of Yuma Dean. Priest started to cough.

Most likely started this way for Gramps, smelling things that had no smell, and gagging on them.

The other two bedrolls lay stuffed with clothes and were supposed to look as if Jowett and Lamarr were asleep. Lamarr had stuck his yellow sombrero out the top of his blankets, like he might be wearing it while he slept. Priest was worse than bait, and he felt as doomed as a Judas goat staked in the open to trap bear.

When the shooting started he slipped into the shadows, pressed himself behind a group of boulders, pulled the Colt Lightning revolver, and waited. In ten minutes Lamarr gave him an "all's clear" whistle and Priest moved warily back into the light of the flames.

They had only one sentry, and they led him out of the darkness with the lasso around his neck, hands untied. Jowett held a Smith & Wesson American .44 covering the prisoner. Priest holstered his gun, hating how it felt in his hand and wanting to relieve himself of it as quickly as possible.

"*Hola,* José," Lamarr told Braulio's man, "how about if you just plant yourself in front of the fire right now? If you don't trouble us none, we'll give you some tortillas. They a bit too chewy but pretty filling once you get 'em down."

"I want nothing from you."

"Just tryin' to be a good Christian."

Jowett squared his shoulders. "Now, seat yourself."

"You killed Juan."

"He didn't give me much choice," Jowett said, sounding almost fatherly. "You think if I hadn't gotten the drop on him I'd be here right now? He'd'a put two in my back."

"This was not needed. We were here only to lead you back to the pueblo."

"I don't suppose you were aiming to take the money for yourself. Is that right?"

"Don Braulio's men do not steal from him and live."

"How far are the rest of your amigos?" Lamarr asked.

"Not far."

"I was hopin' for a more exact answer, José."

"My name is not José. I am Ignacio."

"And here I was thinkin' you looked like a José. But now that I take a bit of a gander at you, I see I was wrong. You are an Ignacio."

Lamarr loosened the lasso and drew it free from the lookout. Ignacio's neck had a bullet graze, and the wound was pink and raw. His seared flesh had melted into a fusion of powder burns and black, crusted blood.

He was only a year or two older than Priest, handsome, with blazing deep-set eyes and hair that coiled and curled the way that most women liked. Tall for a Mex, over six feet, rangy, with large hands. His clothes and fingernails were clean. He took pride in his looks. Priest guessed that meant there were plenty of women in Braulio's town, just like Lamarr had said.

With a flourish, Jowett stepped in close. He tried to present himself as more imposing than he was, dangerous and strong and not a bit old. "How many men does Braulio have?"

Ignacio hesitated, looked furtively around. "More than you can handle."

"Son, you let us worry about the handling part, *comprendes*? How many?"

"There are more every week. Perhaps two hundred."

Jowett lashed out with his quirt and brought it down across Ignacio's face. The Mexican yelped and spit blood. Jowett said, "You wouldn't be lying to us now, would you, son?"

"I tell the truth. And I hope you go to the village and find out for yourself."

"How's this Braulio treating my friend?"

"I do not know. I have not seen him."

"If he's dead, then say so."

"I can tell you only that I have not seen him."

"What's Braulio been going around saying then? He sounds to me like a man who spouts off to his people."

"On this he says only that some gringos are bringing money soon. He plans a feast."

Lamarr said, "Well, then, guess we need to get gussied up, seeing as how we're the intended guests of honor."

The downdrafts whistled and whined. Priest put up his collar against the sudden cold, which felt like dead fingers tickling the back of his neck. "I don't reckon he intends to feed us." Turning to Ignacio, he opened his hands in a gesture of friendship. "We just want to turn over the loot, grab the man Braulio's taken, and get the hell out. We're not looking for any trouble. Anything you can help us with to that end?"

"You sound like a fool," Ignacio told him with sadness. "You talk with no understanding of what you have already done, where you are, or what you are heading for."

"So fill me in. How many men are in the second line of sentries?"

"Four."

"How do we get by them without causing a ruckus?"

"You can do it easily. They will be drunk and sleeping. They arise only when Juan and I wake them in the afternoon."

"Did you help them shoot up Willie Landay?"

Ignacio stared at him without comprehension. "I've lived at this pueblo for six months. My father's farm was raided twice by the army and we were starving. My parents died before we found safety. My brother and sister and I, we survived thanks only to Don Braulio." His words were framed as if he were being thankful, but there were bitterness and resentment beneath them.

"You hate him."

"He is worse than the worst man you have ever met."

"You ain't met everybody I have," Lamarr said.

"It does not matter. He is far worse."

So sure of what he was saying, so utterly

convinced. Priest fought back against a shiver. "Then why don't you leave? You don't sound like you want to be a part of what he's got to offer."

"He has food. It is why I and many of us are here. It is why my brother, Juan, was here as well. And my sister, Lucha. There is much death here, but there is also life."

"And women," Lamarr said.

"Yes, and there are many *muchachas* as well. They come for a chance at life. We all do. And some find only the grave. Or worse."

"Same anywhere," Jowett said and raised his .44, leveling it at Ignacio's chest, steady and firm without any hesitation as Priest's hand flashed out and snatched his pistol from him.

"We're not going down that road," Priest said.

"And what do you expect we do with him? Let him go tell his amigos about us? So that we ride into a whole mob of bandits?"

"We're going to give him some money and let him ride out of here."

"You really are crazy."

"Call 'em as you see 'em, old man."

Jowett let out a deep, rumbling breath that went on longer than it should have. "I don't mind tangling on occasion, but I'm a tad busy at the moment, McClaren." He slid a hand into his vest, eased out a streamlined Smith & Wesson pocket .32, did his little turn again so that Priest was smoothly blocked, and shot Ignacio in the throat.

The Mex warbled a cry and whimpered, "*Madre . . .*" Went down on one knee and tried to rise, fell over onto his side, holding tightly to his neck. His boot heels continued sliding against the stone. He reached out and his hand closed around nothing, unclenched, and tried again.

The fear brimmed in his eyes, alive and writhing as he started to crawl. He died hunched over like a terrified animal.

"You rotten son of a bitch!" Priest shouted, and dove on Jowett. Letting it out, letting it all go at last. He reached for his knife and found it gone, grabbed for Braulio's blade and discovered it was missing, too. Lamarr had taken them, knowing what was about to come.

He barely registered the fact that he was still holding on to the .44, but instead of using it he threw the pistol aside, disgusted. "Bastard! Yellow bastard!"

Priest drew back his fist and smashed Jowett in the chin, punched him again, two, three times, slapping him now, backhand, the way you did to someone you had no regard for.

Then Lamarr had him around the waist and was pulling him along the slippery rock. He howled in a voice that wasn't his father's, but also wasn't his own. "Let me be, damn it!"

You did the best that you could for as long as you could and after that, you gave in to whoever you truly were.

Priest broke free again and started forward as Jowett held out his .32 again and gave a bloody grin. "Hellfire, son!" He slobbered a mouthful of blood and started to laugh. It must've made him feel young again, but his exuberance was bound to end soon. "Haven't been in that kind of fray for some little while. Either of you ever lay a hand on me again and I'll kill you both."

"You're all noise," Priest hissed, and turned his back to Jowett, daring him to come on. "Oblige me whenever you like."

He spent the next hour building a cairn over Ignacio's body, carrying the heavy rocks from piles along the rim of the shelf. He thought of all that planed cedar at home and was struck by the fact that he finally had somebody to build a coffin for and couldn't even do it.

* * *

Priest slept for a couple of hours after that, and when he awoke at dawn he found his knives back in his belt, the cairn completely removed, and the body of Ignacio gone.

He didn't know what Lamarr had done with the corpse and only now understood how ludicrous his efforts had been in the first place, leaving the stone-covered grave out in the open along the only trail through the canyon. Crazy all right. And for all of his antics, not even caring a bit about Ignacio's brother, Juan, hidden up there someplace in the rocks.

How righteous could Priest be to act like that?

Not very. Lamarr said nothing. Jowett gave him sidelong glances, some small fear written into his smug features. At least Priest's actions had done that much—made the man unsettled enough to realize he didn't always know just what to expect. That he wasn't in control of this ramble.

An hour after sunup they were out of the canyon and on a rolling high plateau where the land broke out into widespread pastures of lush grass. They passed four sleeping men and Priest could see that Jowett was unsure of how to play it since he'd already so carelessly murdered others. Did you just keep taking lives for the sake of your convenience?

"Let's go," Lamarr said, a little louder than usual. His horse kicked over several empty mescal and pulque jugs. "Lightning could strike on top of them and they wouldn't know it."

Jowett waited for the men to stir, and when they didn't he appeared a touch glum. He thought about it another minute, just to annoy Priest probably, before he spurred his sorrel on into a trot.

There was a certain amount of satisfaction that Priest got from seeing the bruises on Jowett's face, but not as much as he might've hoped for. He kept noticing something there that he wasn't sure about. It had to do with the real reason why he'd come with them in the first place. Not because he was friends with Septemus, but to repay a debt that was due.

Noises from the pueblo flowed along on the breeze. Horses stamping, hammering, pottery clinking together being cleaned in the troughs, rowdy laughter, men yelling amiably, and quieter female voices speaking in Spanish. An infant wailing.

Time for Lamarr to pull one of his fancy tricks. He gave Priest the wide smile that said they were about to do another damn half-witted thing but baby Jesus was with them, well some of the time anyways, and maybe they'd come through this, one way or another. He could tell you a lot with his teeth.

He rode off to a clump of greasewood, came back a few minutes later with his sombrero tightened under his chin.

Jowett said, "All this excitement give you a kick in the bowels, boy?"

"You know how it is, Cap'n. I just a nervous hen on the inside."

They cantered into the central plaza, passing dun-colored deteriorating structures that blended with the ground. The whitewashed walls, red tile roofs, and clusters of outbuildings and corrals reminded Priest of Septemus's ranch. Maybe Braulio was trying to pattern himself after the richest man north of the border.

It wouldn't take long doing business with Septemus before you learned the cards were always stacked against you, and you had to plan bigger and bigger swindles just to stay in the game.

Ignacio had been right, they were planning a feast. There were several fire pits dug in the corners of the square. Elaborate tapestries hung from the buildings; and leather chairs and fine mahogany tables had been placed outdoors in the smaller piazzas. Vaqueros lounged with their bandoleers and rifles on display. Men and women dressed out deer, goat, and quail.

Priest saw a small, wild orchard bearing the last fruit of the season.

Looked like plums.

He had to fight the wave of the past from rising over him, hearing Sarah's voice as it swept him along, like always, back to the shadow of the saguaro. He brought his hand to his hair, thinking of how she'd stroke his temples and squeeze plum juice onto his tongue.

Lamarr said, "Don't eat the fruit if they offer any."

Jowett nodded. "Only grows like that on the bones of dead men. Guess we know where they plant the bodies now."

"Really?" Priest asked, his memory splintering away. "My God."

The men of the village bristled, watched warily, and slid their weapons into their laps.

"We're causing some commotion," Lamarr said.

Jowett smiled amiably at several of the Mexican women, tipped his hat. "Must be the way you smell."

"I tend to think it's your silly pants. Nobody here can believe a man would wear such things."

"That right?"

Priest stared at the villagers wondering which woman was Lucha. When she learned that both her brothers were dead she'd come at them with a machete.

"Looks like a hospitable cantina over there. Let's go wait this sortie out."

"You and your waiting. It's no wonder the slave hunters never got hold of you. You've got more forbearance than Lincoln in his grave."

With his hand out, the way you'd offer it to someone you loved but couldn't stand, Lamarr said, "I think you taken a shine to me. Tell the truth now, you're wishin' you were my daddy, ain't you?"

Jowett swelled indignantly. "Like hell."

"I know you just foolin' now."

They made their way across the courtyard to the cantina's promenade, which rose up in levels and stone staircases along the inner walls of the plaza. Priest hadn't been expecting the pueblo to be so well fashioned and large, teeming with folks. He'd imagined a bandit's sanctuary to be little more than a few adobes and a lot of tents. Instead, they'd found the beginnings of a thriving town.

They tied their horses and sat at a table while everyone else looked on. Jowett, the saddlebags hanging over his shoulder, leaned back and lit a cheroot.

"Guess that's our boy," he said, aiming his chin.

Don Luis Braulio, master of the pueblo, who rustled cattle, peddled small arms and ammunition, and seized caravans, sat with his lieutenants at a huge table piled with roasted goat and frijoles, in a covered area of the cantina set half a floor above the rest of the place.

Priest studied the man's bright, cruel eyes, his long mustache tapering out so wide that it nearly reached his earlobes. Braulio wore his coarse black hair long. Maybe five and a half feet tall, right around the size and build of Septemus. He may have gotten wealthy quickly, but you could tell the money was only a part of what really mattered to him. Anyone who liked to use a slow knife on his enemies had other reasons for doing so than easy cash.

Figures began to filter into the cantina and seat themselves about, blocking escape. Priest didn't worry about it. If the Mexicans had wanted to, they all could've rushed in and made a grab for the money, caused a shoot-out. A dozen or so dead men for twenty thousand. Life was cheap everywhere, but a lot more of a bargain south of the border.

The air was strong with the smell of splashed mescal and pulque. Someone whispered in Braulio's ear and he nodded but didn't turn to look at the newcomers.

So, he was another one who enjoyed building up the show. Short men loved theater. No wonder Braulio sat up there on a stage.

"How about we get us a few *cervezas* 'fore we parley?"

"We're here to do business," Jowett said.

"First rule of business is to make the other man come to you, ain't that true?"

Jowett cocked his chin. The bruises on his face had darkened into angry smears of black. "And what would you know about it?"

"A thing or two, I might say." Lamarr smiled at the nearest girl and she dawdled over uncertainly, trying to flash dimples. He spoke quietly, as if he were saying something private, maybe sweet, and handed her a couple of coins. *"Tres cervezas, por favor, señorita."* She enjoyed the way he said it and volleyed in Spanish with another woman at the bar, then drifted off to get the beer.

"Seems he has the same idea," Priest said. "Ignoring us."

"We could always try to get his attention."

"Let's drink a beer first." He felt as if he could get away with drinking just one or two tonight, and not move up to whiskey. But he always felt that way. "You see anything that looked like it could be used as a jail? A cell?"

"Daddy's either long dead or being treated right homey, I'd guess," Lamarr told him, some of the grave emotions working into his voice. A man needs what he hates most in the world almost as much as what he loves. "Our new friend Don Luis Braulio don't appear to be a man with much inclination toward middle-ground feelings. He either do away with somebody or he act the crony."

"He isn't doing either with us so far."

"Sure he is. We among his people, drinking, with these pretty gals serving us. He's sharing with us."

Lamarr was right, and Priest could see it now. The girl returned with the beer and Priest fingered the wooden cup but kept it at arm's length, realizing he couldn't start drinking or he'd go too far, as usual.

Lamarr sipped his beer, and when he finished, Priest pressed his cup toward him and Lamarr drank that one, too.

Jowett raised an eyebrow but said nothing. He grew lost in scrutinizing the layout of the pueblo, glancing here and there at the people preparing for their feast. He took note of the buildings, the store-houses, the orchard, and the corrals of stolen horses. He looked as if he were trying to resign himself to staying there for a while, and the thought brought a curl of weary bitterness to his lips.

"Let's make our play now," Jowett said.

"If a man ain't in Mississippi he ain't got no reason to live, that what you sayin'?"

"These people are nothing without him. Take him from the picture and the rest will fall in line. I saw it time and again during the war."

"He isn't some fat general on a hill, Cap'n. You draw on him and his men will unload on us for the sheer fun of it."

"Go on," Jowett ordered, with a firmness in his voice, telling an insubordinate to do his duty. "I'll cover you."

"Imagine," Lamarr said. "An ex-slave, ex-Union soldier unwilling to accept the word of a slave hunter and Reb officer. I must be gettin' too set in my doubting ways. I gonna pray for guidance on this very subject tonight."

Giggling children carried a piñata across the square, dashing about and wrestling each other. Priest noted that the kids were cleaner and better fed than many children they'd seen on their trek the last few days.

He eyed Braulio once more, trying to judge and reason through the bandit's motivations. Finally Braulio turned, met Priest's gaze, and held it.

A hand snaked out from the crowd, touched Lamarr's shoulder. Priest looked over and said, "Oh, hell."

Burial Jones Clay stood there smiling at him, the rowel scar a bright white jagged line across his ebony face.

Lamarr kicked back his chair but remained seated, facing Burial. Sometimes everybody smiled so much you just knew someone was going to die. Lamarr kept grinning and said, "Boy, I thought you was gonna get yourself a fat wife and learn to farm."

"Never did like no enchiladas and corn bread. Besides, ain't many of 'em are fat. They all hungry."

"That's too bad. You recall what I said would happen if I ever seen you again?"

"Yassuh, I do."

"Well, now."

They waited. Burial appeared a mite better off now than he had been the last time they'd seen him, freshly arisen from his comfortable coffin covered in his own blood and filth. He'd oiled his holster so the barrel wouldn't make that soft scratching hiss as it slid free. He wore his fancy black-and-white calfskin vest still, and he seemed proud to be among these people. The sheen of stupidity and relentless arrogance had been burned from him and replaced with an uneasy understanding and mindful attitude.

"You look good," Priest said, and he meant it.

"I knew you were cracked, McClaren, but I didn't suppose you were crazy enough to come all the way down here for a spell of bad trouble. Why would you go and do that?"

"We can't choose our trials."

"Ain't that a fact. We the chosen."

Lamarr carefully took off his sombrero and placed it in his lap. "Why don't you sit awhile with us?"

"So you can ask about Don Braulio and his setup here?"

"Yep," Lamarr said, and ordered another round of beer.

"And why should I?"

"Because we gave you a chance to redeem yourself in the eyes of the baby Jesus."

Burial frowned, knowing he did owe his life to Lamarr, and motioned at Jowett. "Who's he?"

"Oh, don't mind him none," Lamarr said. "He just along so he can feel young and useful in the world again."

The words caused Hatcher Jowett's chin to snap up as if he'd been struck. "Don't let the gray fool you, boy. I've always been twice the man any of you are."

"Not exactly the friendly type, is he?" Burial asked.

"He just frettin' all the years he been away from me and mama. See, this here is my possible daddy, accordin' to his own lips. He come all the way from Mississippi to find me and make amends."

Priest leaned in, shoved his *cerveza* aside. "Braulio and his setup."

"Well, there's about two hundred souls," Burial said. "They were starvin'. Don Braulio feeds them, keeps them safe from the Federales and other waywards."

"How'd you make your way here, and where do you fit in with this outfit?"

"They found me. I stole a horse from some old Mex mama and papa, hadn't even gotten the broken-backed beast two or three miles away before Braulio's ramrods showed up. They tried to rob me, but when they saw I didn't have nothin', they just welcomed me into the fold."

"What do you bring to the table?"

"I've been doin' a little rustlin'. Real little. I ain't much good at it. I help out around here, taught them how to run the cantina right. Steal some bottled liquor when I can.

225

Taught 'em how to gamble the right way. I make a dollar or three off these vaqueros."

"Run girls?"

"No need to. They run themselves. No young lost fillies like before. The women all know why they here. Either to cook or take care of the children or take care'a the men. Sometimes all three."

"Guns?"

"More guns than I ever seen before. Stashed all over. Comin' in and goin' out almost every day. Mexicans are at war all the time. With each other. With the United States. With the Spanish. Everybody. You ain't spent much time this side of the border lately, have you?"

Lamarr answered. "Not for a while, no."

"This country . . . these people . . . the way they live, I ain't used to it."

Priest could sense that Burial wanted to discuss matters further but was scared to do so. Don Braulio's lieutenants and the other men circled, growing a little fidgety, even though Braulio still appeared perfectly calm and unhurried to get his hands on the twenty thousand dollars.

Jowett sat back in his seat, propped his heel against the table leg. "I hear they got a bloody way to keep themselves entertained. That right?"

"For Lord's sake, man, don't talk so loud."

"Guess you aren't in as tight as you thought you might be, eh?"

"Nobody that tight. I never killed no one for sport."

"What about Tuvi?" Priest asked.

"She kill herself, you know it."

"I'd say you lent a hand in the matter."

Burial Jones Clay paused and considered it, growing more edgy. "Maybe what you say is true, but what happened back at *La Fonda del Reyes* got nothin' to do with this right here." Burial looked over his shoulder and wide panic spread out on his open face. He slid out of his chair and stormed past the vaqueros and out into the square, glancing back only once.

"Our host is putting in a personal welcome," Jowett said. "Look lively, children."

Braulio was coming over.

Chapter Eleven

His lieutenants flowed around him like shadows, hanging back by inches, at the ready. The other men and women in the cantina parted and held close to the walls. At home, in a bar situation like this, you'd be able to feel the tension growing, the excitement kicking up all over. But in this place, they took it in easy graveyard stride.

Someone gripped the back of Burial's empty chair and drew it farther out, the way a steward might in a fancy restaurant. Braulio sat, took in Jowett first, then Lamarr, then Priest, beaming the whole time.

"Wine!" he called, and after some scurrying they brought it to him in a silver goblet.

He drained it in a single swallow, and they filled it for him again. Priest tried to make out the men's faces but they faded, second by second, into one another. Despite all their attending, service, and waiting on, they simply didn't matter. When Braulio died, they'd vanish back into the hills. They counted now only as an extension of their master.

A mariachi band began to play softly out in the plaza. The girls swayed and danced, the men laughing, cheering. They certainly were a more well-mannered bunch than the folks frequenting most of the saloons in Patience.

"You have the eyes of a ghost, my friend," Braulio said to Priest.

"That so?"

"Yes, and I know of what I speak."

Without doing anything much, Priest somehow always drew malevolence toward him. He was a little taken aback by Braulio's perfect English. There was no trace of an accent, and he realized right off that he'd already underestimated the man. It was always wrong to equate cruelty with ignorance.

"Have you met with many ghosts, Don Braulio?"

"Yes, in the village where I was born. My father called on me when I was a boy and spoke to me for years after he was dead."

"But no more?"

"After I killed my first man, my father stopped visiting. Perhaps he was ashamed of me." He drew his fingers through his long, coarse black hair, the way a kid might do to remind himself of how a parent had once shown affection.

"Anybody else haunt you?"

"One other comes regular, during the quarter moon. A Yaqui I shot in the Sierra Madres a long time ago. He must have been a magic man. He bears no grudge." The sunlight slashed across his brow. "And neither do I. Did you kill my lookouts?"

Priest's lips flattened and his face filled with regret. He reached over to where a half-full cup of beer sat in front of Lamarr and tossed it back in two pulls. Lamarr gave him a disappointed expression—not because of the drinking, but because Priest never had much of a poker face and tended to give away the barn.

"So, it saddens you, what happened to my men, eh? This is strange. I rarely deal with men who feel remorse, and here you've traveled all these miles to meet with me." Braulio held out his arms in camaraderie and clapped Priest on the shoulders. "It's all right. Since you made it past them they would have to die anyway, the same as the other drunken guards."

"What?"

"They failed in their duty."

"Wait. You did them in?"

"They will soon be hung in the square, if you wish to visit." Braulio drank more wine, and when it dripped down his neck, he took off his bandanna and dabbed himself clean. And still no word about the money or Septemus.

"Why are you here, *gringo* child? There is something about you I like very much, and something else I think I very much despise."

"Sounds about right. I seem to bring that about in most folks. Especially women."

Braulio broke into riotous laughter and translated for his men, who also guffawed. Lamarr smiled, too, letting it all ride.

"We have many *chichi muchachas* here. Take whichever one you want, she will be yours during your stay. I demand that you and your friends have a memorable time."

Lamarr allowed his features to twist into a smirk of pure appreciation. "I always did feel proud to meet a man of generosity."

"That I am," Braulio admitted. *"Más vino. Las señoritas, tratan a estos hombres bien, Délos lo que él desea."*

The ladies immediately hovered around the table and pushed their way in. One sank into Lamarr's lap and began to lick his ear. He said, "My, I could get used to this here village. It saddens me some that I ain't stopped by a whole lot sooner."

The other girl appeared too proud to play at this, perhaps angry at being forced to answer Braulio's call. She couldn't bring herself to smile at Priest, and would only touch his shoulder, pretending it was a sign of affection.

Braulio frowned at her and fury bled into his face. Priest waved him off and said, "See what I mean about me and women?"

He kept expecting Jowett to explode at being ignored, but the captain handled it just fine, biding his own time. He drank his beer and didn't hide the stuffed saddlebags or offer them up. He had become so passive that Priest couldn't see the same man who'd walked into Lamarr's place and started knocking clumps of dirt from his heels anymore. There it was again—the feeling that Jowett was hiding something else beneath his usual baseness. Now his stillness.

"Don Luis is right," the girl told Priest. "You do have the eyes of *una spectra*."

"That's just my lack of natural charm showing through."

"It is sadness."

"He just sentimental," Lamarr put in. "He's homesick is all. You get him too far away from his own little acre and he become downright rueful."

"You love too much," Braulio said to Priest. "And you love what is wrong for you."

That stopped him. Was he that far out of control that everybody could read him in a minute or so? He had to start taking charge, learn how to get the look out of his eyes.

"Is that what ghosts do?" he asked, and immediately regretted it. He sounded like an idiot, taking conceit in being like the dead.

"I love nothing. I fear nothing because I love nothing."

"I wouldn't go that far," Priest said. "You love being the center of attention, Don Braulio, same as Septemus." There, putting the name out. "The two of you enjoy entertainment and building up the moment."

Braulio turned it over for a few seconds, stroking his mustache as if he hated it, leaning back in his chair. "You are right, *gringo,* I do adore my amusements. But that is not the love we are talking about. It is different from the distractions that keep us a few steps ahead of our worst misery."

"Heard about a few of them," Lamarr said. "Those there distractions."

"Is that so? And what is it they say?" Knowing exactly what they said, and taking pleasure in the fact.

"Well, there's a padre who buried an old woman a couple of weeks ago who don't have many charitable feelings about you. Of course, he ain't been on the welcoming end of your generosity neither."

"Perhaps he will be one day," Braulio told him, and the threat was implicit and clear.

"Is Septemus Hart alive?" Priest asked.

Don Luis Braulio, master of the pueblo, scowled and said, "Come, let us go to my home where we can speak in private."

"Send those two ahead," Jowett said. "I've got a few things I'd like to discuss first with you, Don Braulio."

"All right," Braulio said without hesitation. "*Vamos!* Escort these men to the house," he ordered, and dismissed Priest and Lamarr.

The vaqueros motioned for them to follow. Lamarr took up his sombrero and put it on his head again, tightened the strap. Priest looked back at the girl, who watched him with compassion and irritation before drifting back to the bar.

* * *

As they were ushered across the plaza by six of Braulio's men, Lamarr said, "I don't think we handled that situation exactly right."

"I'd say that's fair guesswork on your part."

"And furthermore—"

Priest stopped and the Mex behind him walked into him, let out a curse but didn't draw his gun. "Did you just say 'furthermore'?"

"I reckon I did."

"It ain't as sweet as 'perfume of plunder' but it'll do under the circumstances."

"And furthermore," Lamarr continued, "it's becomin' pretty apparent to me that Cap'n Hatcher Jowett knew a whole lot more about this predicament we got here than he let on."

"You think he might be selling Septemus out?" Priest asked. There was bad blood there, the question remained how deep it ran. He was having a hard time putting the pieces together, and the child had begun to talk to him again, whispering in such a way that Priest leaned his head to one side, trying to listen. "Cut a deal with Braulio somehow? Keep the money and become his new partner?"

"In Mississippi?"

"I haven't thought it all the way through yet."

"We have an unfortunate habit of doin' that, in my opinion."

"I know. It'd be nice to have just one correctly laid out plan one of these days."

"We'll keep workin' on it." Lamarr's hands didn't waver near his sash or his Navy .36s, but Priest knew he was thinking about them just by the way he flexed his fingers. "There's only six of them. Think we ought to disarm 'em, run back in the cantina, shoot the place up?"

"Grab the girls and the money, then ride back home again."

"Well, no, first we stop in at the Bird Cage, I'm thinkin'."

"Then we'll lose the girls and the money."

"Some men ain't meant to have much."

"We still have our guns. They didn't even bother to disarm us."

"I guess they know how well you shoot. Still, it's a bit vexin', ain't it?"

They were led across the pueblo to the edge of the orchard, where a large and well-made house rose from the land. Carpenters were still constructing areas of the building, and other vaqueros stood guard on every side.

"Every king needs a castle," Lamarr said.

Priest's eyes narrowed. The dwelling was similar to Septemus's main house on his ranch, but smaller. "I'm starting to think this may be a fixation of some sort."

Somebody shoved a whiskey bottle into his hand. These folks certainly knew how to take care of their visitors.

The vaqueros laughed, ushered them into the home, and then retreated. They didn't lock the door behind them. It was a living room stuffed with Braulio's plunder—stolen European furniture, elegant dining tables, candlesticks, antique vases, silverware, and lidless crates crammed with gorgeous china. Trunks and packing boxes of all sizes. A lot of the goods were broken and had bullet holes marring the wood and packaging.

"Got himself a right little store here," Lamarr said, "if he ever wants to go straight and open a shop in Patience."

"A warehouse. Guess this is what they don't have immediate use for but don't want to give up."

They continued through the home, checking rooms, finding most to be heavily laden with booty. They came to a locked door and Lamarr called, "Yoo-hoo!"

"Get me out of here, you black bastard!" Septemus Hart cried from within.

Lamarr braced his shoulder against the

door and threw himself forward. It took three tries before he finally busted through. Priest heard a soft metallic ringing and the child began to tell him something.

Septemus Hart sat there in one of the huge mahogany chairs, dressed in black trousers and vest with a purple shirt, drinking wine. He wore a gray Rebel coat with gold epaulets, medals, and tassels on it. He'd also been a captain in the Confederate Army and still enjoyed dressing up and showing off the chevrons on his sleeve, using his hanging drawl of an accent when it benefited him to appear as a good ole boy. Even under the circumstances, he did his best to appear stately and suave, detached but polished, refined and implacable.

He barely broke five and a half feet, but he was solid muscle packed with nerve and controlled hostility. You didn't build, own, and keep a city like Patience unless you regularly fought for it and always won. The firelight glinted off his brass buttons and medals and the sheath of his Confederate saber, which angled out from beneath the table.

Septemus was beaming, and you knew immediately that he was Lamarr's daddy, because he had as many teeth in his head as Lamarr did, and they were all just as big and white. He never dropped the smile for a second, and everything he said had that chortle running through it.

Lamarr had no trouble walking right up to him, wearing the yellow sombrero and grinning, waiting patiently.

"What the hell you two been doing?" Septemus asked. "Jawing and drinking, I expect."

"Daddy! I done missed you mightily!" Lamarr held out his arms to give Septemus a great bear hug, and Septemus froze for a second, then held up his saber.

"They let you keep a sword?"

"They act like I'm a guest. Have you killed him yet?"

"Who?"

"Braulio, of course!"

"Not just yet."

"You stupid sons'a bitches."

"We thought we'd turn the money over to him and try to get you out safe and cozy-like, have us a nice trip back across the border. Picnic along the way."

"You should've gunned him down while you had the opportunity."

"We didn't have much of a chance, seeing as how we on a pueblo with two hundred of his men."

Septemus ran a hand through his hair, fidgeting and stomping around restlessly.

Priest slowly moved toward him without fully meaning to do so, getting closer so that he could look down at the man and try once again to see exactly what Sarah could love in him that she couldn't find in Priest. He wanted to ask if it was true that she was pregnant, but the child continued to give him a warning he couldn't make out.

"Something's wrong," Priest said.

Lamarr perked up. "What's that?" Then, staring down, "Did you drink the whole bottle?"

Priest checked and sure enough, the entire bottle of whiskey was empty. "I guess so."

"Oh Christ," Septemus said. "Just what we need now, a drunkard making a bigger mess of things."

"Now, now, Daddy."

"Go outside and kill Braulio now, before he makes us all run that blasted gauntlet of his. He's hell on horseback with those knives!"

"You've got a sword," Priest said. "Why didn't you run him through?"

"He's just waiting for me to try so he can cut my throat."

"Why would he wait to do that? Why didn't he just kill you from the first? And why'd he ask for so little?"

"Twenty thousand isn't some insignificant amount, you idiot. It's more than the two of you are worth plus ten generations after."

"Small enough for an entire pueblo."

"You simpletons," Septemus sighed with a touch of sadness.

The child told him to look, and Priest did. He spotted a key on the floor. That was the metallic sound he'd heard. The door hadn't been locked from the outside but from within. Septemus had locked himself in while Priest and Lamarr had wandered about the house.

He was eager to kill Braulio.

Hatcher Jowett had been too, in the cantina.

"He wanted to cover us," Priest whispered.

Lamarr knew better than to shuck him off when he was like this. "Say again?"

"He would've shot us in the back. Jowett." He spun on Septemus, who was back in his chair and calm again. Laughter drifted in from outside, the vaqueros marching around, starting early on their feast.

Braulio and his lieutenants entered. Septemus pointed and said, "Your setup ain't worth spit to me, the way you run it, Don Braulio. These men waltzed right in here and tried to kill me. If you want back

into my good graces, take them outside
and get rid of them now."

Priest and Lamarr were stripped of their
weapons and shoved across the square
while the people looked on. Braulio stared
at the knives Priest had been carrying. He
held his own throwing blade out and
flipped it across his fingers with ease. It
stood straight up in his palm, the point
down against his skin, and with a slight
movement he tossed the knife around his
wrist until he held it tightly again in his
hand.

The presentation reminded Priest of the
gunslingers who did all kinds of fancywork
with their pistols before they finally shot a
man in the belly. "So, you are a spy, eh?
Sent to murder me with my own blade?"

"No," Priest said.

"And this is why you are a ghost . . . you
knew you would come here to die."

"I'm still hoping against it."

"Who paid you to assassinate me and my
compadre?"

"You got this all at cross angles. We've
been used. So have you."

"Septemus Hart is your own boss, no?"
Braulio asked. "And you betray him. A traitor is no better than a mad animal."

"Our boss?" So that was how Septemus had hoodwinked him. "What did he tell you?"

"That you are from his ranch in the north. And now you come to claim his life so you can take over for yourself. His friend, Señor Hatcher Jowett, heard you scheming. He stopped you from trying to take the money on the trail up the mountains, is that not so?"

"No, that's not so. What's the cash for?"

"It is what is owed me from our past dealings."

"It's blood money. He paid it because he wanted us to finish you off and for you to get rid of us."

"Silence, traitor!"

They came to the four dead guards whom Braulio had hanged for sleeping on duty. Their beaten bodies were crusted with flies and dried blood, and the ropes creaked in the breeze. Their boots and coats were gone. Members of their families kneeled nearby, praying and weeping, the kids staring blankly. Farther along they heard shouting, men firing guns in the air.

"They all excited now," Lamarr said beneath his breath.

"I'm a bit less so."

"Oh, I don't know. My heart is pumpin'

away. I can't wait to see Daddy and the Cap'n again."

"We really are stupid."

"That's a sad fact. We easily misled."

A young woman rushed over and tried to claw at Priest's face. He fended her off and recognized the dead man, Ignacio, in her face. This must be Lucha, his sister.

She hissed in Spanish and kicked at him while the men roared. Funny how the world could turn on you so damn quick. Or maybe it had been slowly twisting this way for a while now, and he'd been too blind to see it.

At the other end of the plaza Braulio had a little setup similar to Septemus's theater—several levels of stadiumlike seats and one special chair at the edge of the common. This was Don Luis Braulio's throne, where he'd sit back after throwing his knives and watch his prisoners bleed out across the red dirt.

"My, my," Lamarr said. "Not just them fancy tiny blades. He got himself some machetes lined up."

Lamarr and Priest were shoved forward with the butts of rifles and forced to go on alone. They walked slowly out into the stone courtyard, which burned and glowed, the air cooked to a heavy heat

245

shimmer. The withering flowers along the walls still had some blossoms, and the hot breeze carried their scent along with the ashes from the cooking fires.

Some of the people were horrified and kept their fists clenched to the center of their chests. Others appeared excited, drunk, hungry for this kind of action.

"I was kind of hopin' they'd applaud and cheer," Lamarr said. "Them pretty girls come down here to us, cryin', holdin' out a handful of daisies."

"That how you see dying?"

"I don't see the dyin' part rightly, just the pretty girls, tears in their big, beautiful eyes, sweat gleaming on all that nice golden brown skin, holding out armfuls of roses, swingin' their personables—"

But Priest did see the dying part. His corpse being dragged away by the feet, hung up in the center of town where the men would laugh and the children would use sticks to crack open his skull, and the crows could peck him down to the bone. The thought infuriated him. He still had a lot to do.

"You think we can make it?" Lamarr asked.

"Yep, if he doesn't cheat."

"I always try to make an effort to believe in a man's natural worth and honesty.

Mama said we have to make the Christian effort."

"That's why we're easily misled. Amazing how you black folks have such a good-natured outlook on life, considering you were stuck on the plantation and all."

Lamarr kept turning it around, trying to figure out how the setup had been rigged, his lips working and his brow furrowed. Priest realized that Lamarr had truly been hoping to save Septemus so that he could have the man be in his debt. Now he had no edge on his father again.

"So Daddy wants us to rid him of Braulio and keep his own hands clean. Doesn't even have to pay his men on the ranch any extra wages for putting their lives on the line."

"Gets his killin' done for free by us."

"And nobody on the pueblo or back home in Patience even suspects him much 'cause they know we ain't ever gonna work for him."

"No, not the two men who hate him most."

Lamarr pulled another face. "I still can't see it all the way to the other end. No matter how good a bandito pack these men might make, there can't be enough money here to interest my daddy."

"It's got to be political. Maybe Septemus

cut a deal with the Federales. Running guns. These people fight more wars than we can keep track of. He keeps Braulio and the others out of the way of the Mexican officials, and they promise him protection. Favors. Kickbacks."

"And the Cap'n?"

"Him I have no idea about. Why would Jowett come all the way down here to run a village like this? Nothing but hungry Mexicans and vaqueros. You heard him on the trail, he couldn't talk about anything but Vicksburg."

"And he sure was talkin' downright nasty about Daddy. I don't think they get along much."

"So Septemus has something on Jowett and is using him to his own ends. Keeps him down here for a few months in charge of stealing cattle and guns for him, his man in north Mexico. How long do the vaqueros keep him alive before one of them takes a run at him?"

"Not long at all," Lamarr said. "A band of Braulio's lieutenants would decide pretty quick to grab the whole business for themselves."

"Of course, and they have to know it'll happen that way. Braulio is cruel, but it would take somebody like that to keep so many other banditos in line."

"Our good Captain Hatcher Jowett must be in deep for Septemus to ring the dinner bell like this on him."

"You fear losing only what you love," Priest told him. "That's what Braulio said."

"More or less."

"So what's Jowett love?"

" 'Sides them silly pants?"

"He's never mentioned a wife. He hiding something?"

"Septemus gonna take his wife away from him?"

"Or his spread."

Lamarr let out a lengthy, sorrowful sigh. "Sad to see former comrades turn on each other like that, I must say. Why, if I was a gambling man—"

"Which isn't to say you are."

"That's true, but if I was, then just about now is when I'd be expectin' Molly and Chicorah's men to come riding down to save us. Why, if you look close out there, I bet you can make out their dust right about this minute."

Priest glanced aside, didn't see any dust. "You might have to fold on this hand."

"Damn it. Baby Jesus just testin' our faith a little."

Chapter Twelve

Braulio was the center of attention, as he had to be. He swung toward his captives, rattling in Spanish. Emphasizing certain statements and then waiting for a response from his people.

Men fired shotguns into the air. A procession of villagers passed out plates of the roasted goat and were served their food and drink. Clay jugs filled with wine went around. They took their seats in the stands, ate, and waited.

The delays and pauses and tarrying were all a part of his show. Braulio left them out there in the sun for a while, thinking some more about what was coming. He shouted across the square and addressed Priest and Lamarr.

"So, you thought you would come here

251

and make a fool of me in my own village. You attempt to kill someone under my protection. And now"—he held up his arms, waiting for his people to give an ovation but receiving only drunken hoots and the clapping of frightened children—"you shall distract us this evening from the trials of life. If you make it to the distant wall, you may climb to freedom."

Lamarr said, "Shoo-ee, and I was just startin' to like him some, too. Man of generosity he was for such a short period of time."

For ten minutes more Braulio toyed with his machetes and his honed throwing blades, juggling the weapons with incredible precision, throwing them in looping, far-ranging arcs and striking pigs on the other side of the plaza.

"Got me a taste for some barbecued spareribs now," Lamarr said.

"So do I, actually."

"You figure he's better with a knife than you?"

"Maybe."

"It's a hard thing to reckon."

More so for Priest than for anybody. "Stay here," he said.

Lamarr grimaced, tilting his chin. "Where am I gonna go? And where the hell are you headin' off to?"

"I want to talk to him."

"I suspect he's beyond listenin'. But please yourself. I gonna stand here and wave to all my loved ones out there." He untied his red sash and beckoned the girls with it.

Priest walked over as Braulio's lieutenants fired into the dirt before Priest's feet. He kept going. Braulio waved his men off, stood there fascinated that Priest would dare come on over.

You had to hand it to the little tyrants, they certainly took themselves seriously.

"You wish to beg for your life?"

"No, not quite," Priest said.

"You intend to appeal to my better nature?"

"Listen—"

Braulio hefted his machete, turned, and called to a boy standing nearby. The kid's mother screamed, and one of the vaqueros viciously shoved her down and slapped her across the face. The boy was no more than seven or eight and was too terrified to even cry. He stared at his fallen mother and held out his hands to her.

"All right," Priest said. "Okay."

"But I have done nothing yet." He grabbed the kid by the hair and hauled his head up so that his throat was bared. Priest figured he could snatch the machete out of Braulio's fist if it came to that, even if the men around him cut him down a second afterward. Braulio grinned at the boy, and so did Priest.

"If you do not run for the distant wall when I say, I will have my men shoot you where you stand."

"Sure," Priest said. "I already said okay. We'll finish our discussion a bit later then."

Braulio blinked at him and his happy leer shifted into a scowl, the mustache bobbing across his face. "You think you can't die like the rest of them?"

"I'm a ghost, remember?" Priest said, and walked back to where Lamarr was waiting. He was still waving to the women, some of whom waved back and threw flowers.

"Don't suppose it went off too well?"

"Nope."

"It was nice of you to think he'd be reasonable considerin' we on a death run here."

"I was hoping to avoid it."

"Maybe you should try again, offer him some peonies this time."

"He'll kill a boy if I do."

The petals fell around them, drifting over and catching in the rim of Lamarr's sombrero. "Oh, well then."

Priest scanned the crowd, searching the

faces. Lamarr tied his sash back around his waist and said, "Daddy and the cap'n ain't nowhere to be seen. Guess they havin' a few drinks of wine at our hefty expense."

"Burial Jones Clay, too, I suppose. I don't spot him in the crowd."

"And I thought I'd turned his heart toward the Lord."

"Guess he's still irate about being left in a coffin for so long."

"Gonna be a mite longer next time, I'm thinkin'."

After watching Braulio hurling knives at the pigs, Priest knew he could make it to the wall, but Lamarr, for all his strength, wasn't much for speed. Somehow Priest had to cover him as they ran. He knew of only one way to do it, and he figured it would turn the game up a notch.

"Guess we should cheat some ourselves, eh?"

"Hell, yes," Priest said. "Even if we get over the wall Braulio's men will just pick us off on the other side." And bring them back hog-tied so they could get their feet chopped off.

Lamarr tightened his sombrero on his head. "Gonna be close."

"We never were much good at playing it

255

any different," Priest said. He had to buy just a little time when they started to run.

Something came to him but he wasn't sure it was possible. Not for him. Priest had seen it happen only once before in his life, with a Chevelon Creek Mescalero named Yellow Dog, showing off before his intended's father, who was one of the Apaches' better advisors. Priest remembered watching Dog's fluid, confident moves, one after the other as he faced three of his beloved's uncles all carrying weapons. Dog moved so fast, almost mystically, that you could hardly see his feet as he ran.

The more he thought about it, the more impossible it seemed. The fact that Dog was dead didn't help any either.

"You remember Yellow Dog?" Priest asked.

"That Mescalero buck? Thought he could outrun the wind."

"Yeah."

"Damn near could."

"But not quite."

"Not in the end anyways. Unwise way to strut and pose, putting on a display like that. Boy had more pride than brains. Girl he was supposed to marry still moons over him, what I hear. And that was what? Two years ago?"

"Closer to three."

"Still, got to allow, he had grit." Then Lamarr caught on and he snapped up straight as if someone had prodded a pistol in his back. Petals fell off his brim and showered his shoulders. The smile came out but no show of teeth. "You think you're faster than the Dog?"

"Maybe so."

"No white man is faster than an Apache. You know that."

"Some of Gramps might be in me, too."

"Meanin' you as off your head as him?"

"Just in case you haven't noticed, we ain't exactly got a mile of options."

"We got one surprise that'll help."

Priest didn't think so. He figured it was about the dumbest thing he'd ever heard that he hadn't thought up himself. "That won't be of any use until we're over the wall."

"I'm startin' to get a little tired here. You think if we ask he'll move it along some?"

"Would've been nice to run into a bandito who cared only about money and not all this sporty showiness."

"You know, I'm startin' to think that the padre mighta had us pegged all the time."

"The worst of fools?" Priest said. "I might be in agreement on that."

* * *

So, it had come down to this. Braulio staring at them, fascinated, perplexed, still trying to reason out why they weren't screaming and kicking up a fuss. Lamarr had courage. Priest didn't know what he had, and wasn't sure he wanted it.

The whiskey in him had started to hit the right spot. Not in his head but someplace further inside, under the heart, where it blunted the edges of the world.

Now Braulio was shouting again but Priest couldn't hear him anymore. Lucha stood on the steps and hissed her hatred. Her malice cut grooves into her face and made her suddenly ugly.

It wasn't much ground to cover, maybe seventy-five yards, a little more. At least it gave Priest an idea of what kind of range Braulio had with his special talent. Lamarr turned and gave him the smile again, wide and happy like this was nothing but a game from the start, and then they were running.

The knives flew after him and the child told him how to move, when to dodge. He kept up the pace and shouldered Lamarr aside when he had to, the two of them weaving this way and that to avoid the machetes and throwing blades.

The breeze brushed down inside of Priest's collar and the scent of the plum trees filled him again. The fruit, like his memories, was growing out of the dead.

"Goddamn!" Lamarr barked, sounding like he was having fun. "That was close!"

This was so damn silly Priest wanted to buckle and let loose with whoops of laughter. He had gone from five years of hating Yuma Dean and seeking to pay back a blood debt to being duped by Septemus Hart and chasing his own shadow across a plaza.

It tickled him some, too, thinking about the entire scene as a bandito hurled murder at him and the villagers looked on in puzzled and helpless complicity.

He deserved to be a part of this ludicrous parlor trick. You got what you earned. He hadn't actually set out to do something heroic, and that's where the fault lay. His mission had been a sham, thinking he would save Septemus and somehow win back Sarah. Rage and his own pettiness had marred his intentions, and the child admonished him for this.

Because his pursuit hadn't been pure, he'd been consigned to this ridiculous contest. Even Lamarr's scorn and need for the old man were at least honest feelings.

The machetes sailed closer as the child

spoke. Braulio had tremendous talent, toying with them at first but now trying harder to nail them.

A throwing knife winged Lamarr's sombrero and he cried out, "My hat! That bastard! Must think he's a barber!"

Priest reached out to lend a helping hand, gripping an elbow and pulling him along. Lamarr fell back a step, then another, and then three, but he kept on smiling.

He wasn't going to make it.

Priest slapped him on the back, urging him to continue, the knives soaring closer and closer.

Yellow Dog had almost pulled it off.

Standing before his beloved's uncles and insulting them, making faces, acting out and enjoying it. So fast you could barely see him moving until he was already in another spot, avoiding the arrow first, then the tomahawk and the stone hammer. Dancing around at ease and feeling so clever, pushing fate a bit too hard, he tried to grab the spear angling toward him out of the air instead of ducking it. He spun aside, reaching, grinning at his bride-to-be as his sleek skin gleamed and the metal point glared in the sunlight, and then Dog was standing there gape-mouthed with the spear sticking out of his chest.

Priest thought back to Patty's place when Gramps had thrown him the knife, the Bible flapping open as it hit Deed's chest, and the pages crinkling softly like a merciful whisper.

Time was draining away again, it always was, and his mother's prayers tumbled through the back of his mind, the child unable to guide his hands but offering him compassion.

He spun and faced the knives.

Two blades came sailing toward him, one at his face, the other lower, at the knee. Maybe it was intentional, Braulio hoping to clip him, cripple him, watch him bleeding and crawling on his belly, hoping to get him to plead. Then, swinging the machete down at the right angle to take off Priest's head with a single blow.

Another half second.

Weapons littered the square. Lamarr was nearly to the wall. Priest's diversion had worked, and he had just enough time to glance over and see the amazement and awe in Braulio's eyes.

Now Priest's right hand flashed out and he snatched the first throwing blade from the air, that balanced handle soaring perfectly into his palm like a bird he had called home.

His left shot out and went for the second

knife, but his timing was a hair off, he just wasn't good enough to do it twice. Oh, Dog, you howling at me? Priest tried to slip aside but the blade skimmed his knee.

Blood began to pour but he didn't feel any pain yet. Lamarr managed to get two steps up the whitewashed wall and, arms outstretched, grabbed the top of it and hung there for an instant before pulling himself up.

Braulio's men were shocked and started to raise their rifles and take aim. Priest watched the second knife skitter into the dust, bent and nabbed it, took off for the wall again. Shots whizzed past. He made it in four strides, was over it and falling before he knew he'd cleared the top.

He dropped and nearly landed on Lamarr, who held his sombrero tightly to his chest. The top two inches had been cut off. Inside were three sticks of dynamite wrapped in sacking.

"That's still the stupidest thing I've ever seen," Priest said. "Far and away."

"You won't be laughing at this here stroke of my genius in another minute." He struck a match and held it to the end of a fuse.

Priest could hear Braulio shouting, the stamp of horses, and the men coming for them now. "Anytime you're ready."

"Uh yeah, well . . . you just wait."

Lamarr tried again but couldn't light the fuse.

"What's the matter?"

"I was sweating too much under my fine hat! The fuses are wet!"

"Christ." Priest grabbed a stick of dynamite and felt the fuse. It was drenched damn near to the bottom. He cut it short.

"That there might be a bit too runty for our needs."

"Light it and run."

"More runnin'? I'm gettin' a little sick of all these steep amounts work with no fun in between."

Lamarr lit another match. The fuse ignited and he threw himself down. Priest flung the dynamite sidearm over the wall just as two of Braulio's men showed their faces. The explosion blew out a part of the wall and the vaqueros screamed and fell from sight. The smell of blood grew strong on the wind. Villagers yelled and shrieked and the hogs squealed wildly.

"You're bleedin' pretty bad," Lamarr said.

Priest checked the wound. "It's okay. Barely scraped me."

"Yellow Dog was surely watchin' over you."

Maybe it was true.

Priest grabbed a stick and ran with it

as fast as he could, heading back to the entrance of the pueblo where they'd first ridden in. He only had a few seconds before Braulio's lieutenants would come storming out of the village. Braulio wouldn't do it himself now that he knew they had explosives.

Priest dropped, cut the wet fuse short, lit a match and waited a three count. As soon as he heard the stamp of horses he hurled the dynamite at the nearest decrepit outbuilding. The blast took out most of the building and showered stone and wood atop the riders. Two men fell into the dust, bellowing in pain. Their sorrels stamped, bucked, and raced past Priest.

They wouldn't try coming out the front gate again so soon.

In a minute he was back beside Lamarr, who held the third stick in reserve. "I've got to admit," Priest said, "now's when the plan gets a little hazy to me."

"We move. It's almost sundown. We can hide in any of these pastures of heavy grass until night. Even those trees afford some protection. Them boys are shaken up plenty and won't try anything for a bit."

Priest didn't see any refuge at all, but if Lamarr said they could do it, then they'd do it. A man who'd hide in a coffin four deep with the dead was bound to know where to find cover.

It took three hours of crawling around in the grass as they avoided the vaqueros' hunting parties before they made it back to the cluster of greasewood they'd passed on the outskirts of the pueblo. It's where Lamarr had hidden the dynamite in his hat. Among the brush he'd hidden a set of Peacemakers and the second .41 Colt Lightning that Priest had asked Molly to give him, in case he lost the first.

Priest slid the two throwing blades into his belt and felt anxious to finish his discussion with Braulio, the way he'd promised.

Darkness settled against them as the torches of the men rushed over the plateau in every direction. On occasion they got so close that Lamarr would clutch the back of Priest's neck and press him down to the earth, keeping him still. The moonlight barely grazed the land.

"We ain't done here yet," Lamarr whispered, his massive hands clenching and unclenching, thinking about his father's neck. There was a mad growl of happiness in his voice. "Not by a damn long sight."

Chapter Thirteen

Lamarr said it was basic battle strategy. While the soldiers were off looking for you, you plundered their camp.

They climbed back over the crumbled section of the wall and re-entered the empty, dark plaza. Lamarr had a new kind of stealth in his stride, or maybe it was an old one returning to him. "Last place they'll look is the first place they lost us."

The night folded in on them. It was so much like the raid on Septemus's ranch several months ago that he felt an overwhelming sense of life repeating itself. Lamarr started humming and Priest had learned enough of the tune to hum along with him. Lamarr had survived chains and war and killed anyone fool enough to try to rob him or brand him or lynch him, and still it all came back to being a fatherless boy. There was protection in his mother's songs.

Priest had to admit he was a little surprised that there wasn't a storm about to break over them. That night at Septemus's ranch a storm had drowned out the noise.

But now the sound of creaking ropes pulled Priest from his thoughts.

Braulio had taken out his anger on more of his men. There wasn't enough moonlight to count the bodies but there were a lot more strung up in the square now, boots knocking against one another.

Lamarr said, "He ain't quite as generous as I was thinkin'."

"We kill him and we play into Septemus's hand."

"Been doin' that since I was born, I reckon. We gonna settle a few debts tonight."

"No guards around."

"Three reasons for that. One is most of 'em are outside the pueblo huntin' us in the brush. Second is he's killed a few more of them and I'm pretty certain more are off packing, ready to finally take their chances anywhere else but here."

"And the third," Priest said, "is because he's inviting us back in to join him."

"Sure. Ignorin' us, same as in the cantina. Ignorin' us but trying to keep an eye on us."

Creeping along, they hung close to the adobes and the pens and corrals. Priest knew they hadn't thought it through enough. They were letting their anger pull them along without regard to consequences, but what the hell.

Priest sucked wind through his teeth. He lurched backward because he'd just stepped on what he knew must be human flesh.

It was the body of the boy that Braulio had threatened earlier. His throat had been cut all the way through so that his head was barely affixed. He'd bled out and the pooled blood had already sunk into the earth. Braulio must've killed the kid moments after Priest and Lamarr had jumped the wall.

A door to one of the huts opened and suddenly there was a burst of motion near them. Lamarr drew and pointed but Priest smacked the barrel of the gun aside with his knife.

Lucha surged forward, appearing demonic in the night, her swirling black hair a dervish in the breeze, and she was holding one of Braulio's machetes. She let loose with a heinous growl that clung inside her chest like a frenzied animal's.

Sidestepping the corpse of the boy, she flung herself at Priest. He caught her gently in his arms and tugged her into the shadows, pressed her face to his chest in a gesture of tenderness and pity. She bit him through his shirt and wouldn't let go until he put the flat of his palm under her chin and pushed her off. Her mouth was full of his blood. They were both gasping and took a few seconds to recover.

"Were you his mother?" Priest asked. She spit at him, and he shook her hard. "Answer me."

"No. He was a beggar, no different from any of us."

"You act like I killed him."

"You did. Him and my brothers."

"I didn't harm your brothers. The other man we rode in with, he did it." Priest was aware of how hollow his own words were, especially since he wasn't sure that Jowett had killed the other man on the ledge. It could've been Lamarr.

"Don Braulio has never been like this before."

"That's not our fault, either."

Her breasts pressed against him and her black fury made him feel even closer to his own death.

Fine, maybe it would end here, but not

before he got to take out his rage on somebody.

Lucha drew back as if aware of his bitter notions. He said, "You live in fear of him every moment. Your brother said he was worse than the worst man alive."

"He feeds us."

"You can feed yourselves."

"What do you know of it? We are starving. All the people here, for miles and miles. Everywhere you go, everyone you meet. Hungry and dying."

"I know there's a group of long-necked men swinging in the square who were Braulio's friends a few hours ago."

"He has no friends."

"Damn right. So why do you defend him?"

"You would never understand unless you had to live the way we do."

"I've done it," Lamarr said. "And had abundant other woes and misfortune, girl. He enslaves you people. I killed lots of men and went to war to stop that kind of trespass. Me and plenty like me."

"You are strong and we are weak. Go, do what you wish. Die by his hand. You will change nothing." She ran back inside her home, shut the door, and blew out the candle. Priest stared after her for a time, wondering if she was right in everything she'd told them.

They left the boy where he lay. They prowled through the shadows across the pueblo and ducked into the orchard, sneaking up to where Braulio's large house stood like a resentful and grieving imitation of Septemus's home. Figures moved behind the windows.

"So how do we play it?"

"We can knock. I know you're big on that."

Priest was so wired he almost didn't catch the reference to the raid on Septemus's place, when Priest had used the heavy brass knocker to announce himself. The hell of it was, he felt like doing it again. Walk in, sit down, talk it out some, and then do whatever needed to be done afterward.

"Light the last stick."

"Now that's my kind of plan. Shoot out the window first; then toss it through."

Lamarr took out the last stick, pulled a match, and perked up when he heard a footstep behind him. In one smooth move he tossed the dynamite to Priest and spun, crouched, and drew.

Three vaqueros bearing lanterns and shotguns called out and Lamarr started shooting. It amazed Priest because, for about the first time ever, Lamarr was stone-faced.

Priest pocketed the stick and took cover against the side of the adobe, drew his own pistol, and fired haphazardly. He couldn't remember a goddamn thing Molly had taught him. He stood all wrong and couldn't get an even, unhindered grip, forgot to hold his breath, and just yanked the trigger.

Two of the men grunted and went over, their lanterns shattering against the ground. Burning oil ran out in bright, irregular patterns of flame. A downward shotgun blast caused a shower of dirt.

"More are comin'," Lamarr said. "I'll take care of them."

"Maybe baby Jesus looks out for fools, but he might have something against being downright asinine."

"You got the bigger job. Just don't kill my daddy."

Priest lit the fuse and tossed the stick at the window, forgetting to shoot it out first. It bounced back at him. He cursed himself, grabbed the dynamite, and aimed his pistol at the glass. He used his three remaining shots and still couldn't manage to break the window out. He wasn't made for guns.

"Okay," he said, walked up to the front door and kicked it in. Bullets smashed into the jamb and splinters flew against the side of his neck. He threw the stick inside, stepped back, and watched the room blow apart.

Screams erupted and Priest grinned, thinking of the dead boy with his throat cut. He gave it a five count and entered the haze of smoke and dying flame. Jowett was on the floor, holding his mangled right leg, writhing, and chewing his lips. Blood spilled out over his fingers and Priest could see the bright white of bone climbing out of the captain's flesh. He felt a surge of pity and didn't know why.

Two more of Braulio's men—without faces—lay dead in a heap on top of Braulio, where he had been holding them up like a shield.

All but one lamp had been blasted to hell, and in its sickly yellow light, Braulio grinned beneath the bodies, coughing, gripping a rifle with a busted stock. His brutal eyes were clear and filled with elation. He threw down the broken rifle and seized a nearby knife, started to work himself free from the dead.

Propped against the wall sat Septemus Hart, dazed from the blast and wearily wiping ash off his face, shaking sawdust from his head of fine white hair. Priest grabbed Septemus by his collar and hauled him to his feet, angled his chin just right, and drove his fist into Septemus's face. Picked him up and punched him again, realizing it wasn't easing his rage any.

Septemus coughed blood and crumpled as Braulio finally managed to stand, took his stance with the blade poised.

"In my soul I knew it was meant to come to this," he said, "from the moment we met."

"Sure," Priest told him.

He felt kind of the same way, and remembered how it had felt when Sarah had first handed him the finely crafted blade and he enjoyed the art, precision, and power that had gone into the weapon.

He took the slow knife out of his belt and held it before him. A flood of pain would follow, that much was clear. And like before, Priest couldn't help chuckling, the scorn moving sinuously inside him.

What would he have done if Braulio had proven reasonable? If the bandit had listened and eventually realized he was being lied to and set up by Septemus? Did the murder of the boy bring them to this point? It wasn't the death run because Priest hardly felt nettled about that at all.

They hadn't been around each other long

enough to truly hate one another, and yet here he was, ready to do another killing. It had taken him five years to hone his hatred for Yuma Dean and do the job. It had taken his love for Miss Patty and his need to protect her in order for him to dispatch the preacher Deed.

But here—now, there was only the overwhelming notion that he was being toyed with by fate to do what should have somehow been averted.

He could make another effort, try a little harder not to be such a damn fool this one time. Priest opened his mouth and Braulio attacked, the blade striking like a snake. Priest parried with his knife, covering himself with vertical and horizontal thrusts as Braulio jabbed again and again.

He had never fought a man in this way before, but the movements came naturally, swiftly, his body moving on its own accord, that much smarter and more self-assured than he was when thinking about it.

Sparks flew as the metal clashed and rang. Braulio reached out with his left hand and tried to choke Priest while driving his blade in close to Priest's belly. Even now he cared more about gutting his prize, leaving him there on the floor with his guts hanging open, a butchered pig for the others to see.

Priest shouted at Jowett and said, "Tell him! Tell him the truth!" Jowett's face was utterly white, and he was too weak even to hold on to his mangled leg anymore, which bubbled blood.

The irony wasn't lost on Priest even while he fought for his life: somehow he cared more about not killing Braulio than he did about possibly having already killed Jowett.

Braulio's thumb slid over, trying to crush Priest's Adam's apple, and Priest shoved his hip out, angling Braulio into the corner of one of the long dining tables.

The edge caught Braulio in the backbone and he let out a yelp. His grip loosened and Priest yanked his throat away, coughing, holding back his insane rage, which wanted to surge. Braulio held his blade low, slicing in sweeping arcs. Priest dodged and slipped out of range, came around to where Septemus was starting to cough and rouse himself once more. Priest kicked him in the face and he went out again.

"Submit," Braulio hissed, "you came here to die. You wish your suffering to end, is it not true?"

"Everyone wants that."

"I have met many like you before."

"That's because you're no different. You've been looking for ghosts over your

shoulder since you were a boy. That Yaqui
magic man you killed in the Sierra Madres
a long time ago. He might not bear a
grudge but plenty of others do." Braulio's
face opened in shock, and he suddenly
seemed young, much younger than Priest.
"They crowd you!"

Priest understood the way Braulio
moved now. He had a particular pattern
of defense and attack, how he thrust, even
how he feigned. Priest got a step ahead of
him and countered easily, until Don Luis
Braulio was gasping for breath and his
lips shifted into a bitter smile of someone
resigned to death and eager to understand it.

"Even this saddens you, *gringo* child?"
he asked. "You do not wish to kill."

"I love too much according to you, and I
love what is wrong for me."

It had suddenly become too smooth and
effortless. Priest had Braulio now, and he
could finish this anytime he wanted. Don
Braulio remained incredibly fast, the blade
moving with amazing speed, but Priest
parried each stroke, the chiming metal re-
sounding like distant church bells.

"If you slay me then all these people go
back to starving in their barren villages."

Priest knew it was true. There were hundreds of folks out there in the pueblo.

Ignacio had said they'd come willingly to the devil because he fed them. And doing it would only be playing into Septemus's plans.

Backing off a step, Braulio lowered his knife, waiting, the sweat dripping along the sides of his face and hanging in his mustache. Priest looked over at Jowett, who said, "Get it done."

This couldn't be blamed on love. Priest turned back, thought of the little beggar boy with his throat cut, the bodies hanging in the square. Septemus's self-indulgent smile, and Sarah when she was weeping. The hate left him. Everything did, until he felt only a cool wind wafting through his mind.

"How much do you weigh?" he asked.

"You ask me this now? You are *loco.*"

"Are you sure of that, Don Braulio?" he asked, his voice sympathetic and plaintive. "Are you so certain? You have the eyes of a ghost, too, now. What do you see?"

With one last desperate, wild charge Braulio attacked, drove his knife much higher than before, at Priest's face, leaving himself wide open.

Priest held his blade out but didn't stab forward—just left it there as Braulio impaled himself on it.

Blood gushed and Priest let go, started to

279

move away, but Braulio jumped at him with arms wide open. Priest held him, patting his back, more or less hugging him close. There had to be mercy.

Braulio stared over Priest's shoulder, the dejected grin slowly dying and dropping from his face as his features folded into a frown. Until, slowly, his eyes filled with dread.

"Father?" he called. "*Padre? Qué usted ahora está haciendo aquí?* Am I to die then? Will you guide your son? *Es usted para eliminarme?*"

So maybe Priest would carry Braulio's soul around on his back for the rest of his life, having killed him with his own weapon. Molly had warned him. He stared into the bandit's face, waiting for the light to dim.

It took awhile as his face softened, filled with contentment, perhaps due to the love of his dead father. Priest lifted the corpse over his shoulder and carried it outside, where Lamarr was still running around the pueblo shooting the place up and keeping the others moving.

The injured lay sprawled everywhere, women and children now peeking out of their doors. Priest walked into the square while the bullets sang past him, threw

Braulio's body out in the dirt, and said, "This devil is dead. If you don't want to feed yourselves, just wait a little while. Another will be along any day."

Chapter Fourteen

Lamarr had been winged and the blood ran in rivulets from his shoulder down along his massive arm. His dark skin was peppered with shot but he didn't seem to mind much. He hauled Septemus up and dragged him over to the dining table, stuck him in one of the lavishly cushioned mahogany chairs.

Priest bandaged Jowett's leg while the man stared at him with a killing gaze. The captain vomited and passed out twice in five minutes. When Priest was done, Lamarr hauled Jowett over to the chair next to Septemus and sat him down, then poured wine into ornate goblets for everybody. He sat at the head of the table and put up his feet, tipped his chin up until his battered sombrero fell off and dropped to the floor, and drank.

Septemus was waking, groaning in his seat. He made little cries of distress and protest. Lamarr sat up and pushed his chalice to Septemus's mouth, forced him to take a swig. It roused him instantly and he held the giant goblet in his tiny hands, sucking from it while Lamarr murmured comforting words like a father. Maybe it's all he'd ever really wanted since he'd killed his plantation owner and started searching for his daddy.

The sounds of weeping floated in through the smashed front doorway. Dim spheres of light from torches and lamps moved across the plaza, this way and that, a gathering of flame that came together and then parted again. Priest glanced over at Jowett and said, "Cap'n," prodding him to speak. "What'd your good friend have on you that he could force your hand to be a part of this?"

Jowett drank, hoping to blunt his torment, but the agony rushed across his face in waves. He gulped more and more wine and Lamarr kept pouring it.

Finally Jowett sat back drunkenly, dulled, and said, "So much of the South burned, but I made it through all right. As a slave-catcher I brought in a fair dollar, and my plantation always turned a profit.

Even after the war I lived on the hog, but then, a few years back . . . I made a few bad business deals."

"My heart does ache," Lamarr said, "for the rich man that falls from grace."

"Took on too much land I couldn't run. Septemus kept me afloat for a time—"

Nodding, Priest eyed the crate with the bottles of whiskey in it, fighting down his thirst. "But you knew he'd eventually call in on the debt."

Septemus, pouting, muttered, "I made good. He had to do the same."

"And I did," Jowett told him. The powder burn scars on his neck stood out bold and ugly as his flesh took on a gray tinge. His self-satisfied smirk had been wiped clean from his face, and all that remained were the vestiges of shame and anger. "You called and I came running."

"You had nowhere else to go but to me. You remember that, Hatcher. You dwell on that damn long and hard."

"Don't think I haven't already."

Priest and Lamarr knew there had to be a little more to it than that, but the story would eventually unravel, one way or the other. Lamarr got into his "praise-Jesus" position, hands clasped together over his heart. "Chums lendin' a helping hand. You two ought to help out at Sunday school, show all the chillun such fine examples of how to lead a Christian life."

"Sister Teresa and Sister Lorraina can always use help with the orphans and the mission," Priest said. His voice had begun to grow thick with his seething, as if he were about to lose himself in a rant, start preaching to the pigs.

"Friendship, tolerance, and consideration, the bonds forged in battle under the Confederate flag. I do believe I'm startin' to feel a longin' to visit the cotton fields of my youth."

"Shut the hell up, you cocky black buck!" Jowett screamed, and Septemus looked more insulted than Lamarr did.

"My, you do have a way, Hatcher," Septemus said, then caught Lamarr's eye. "He took himself a nigger woman for a wife. He don't like to admit he loves her. She lives right up there in his house, to this day."

"Oh Lordy. The disgrace."

Jowett didn't bother to pretend scorn. He sat in his seat, beaten with his own shame, disgusted with himself, drinking even more heavily as spasms of pain made him contort and twist in the chair. "I backed your play, Septemus. Now take me to a doctor and let me go home."

"Gangrene will take that leg before you get back across the border."

"My leg," Jowett panted through his pain, "but not my life." Drops of sweat stood out on his forehead and the anguish made him swoon. Lamarr stood and picked him up in his arms. "Let go. Let me go 'fore I set you out on the lynching tree."

"You come on with your rope and your tar and your feathers and whatall else you got to bring. I'll be waitin' on you. That's all right now."

Priest stared intensely at Septemus across the table, and after a moment glanced at Lamarr. "Give me a few minutes alone with him."

"You ain't plannin' on takin' care of my half-pint daddy all by yourself, now are you? That would upset me some, not being in on that good fun. You ain't got heavy thoughts aimin' that way, do you?"

"No," Priest said, the word sounding like a dismissal, a challenge. Would Lamarr press him? Call him a liar?

"I'll show the cap'n to his quarters. He about to go to sleep on us for a while."

After Lamarr carried Jowett down the corridors to one of the vaulted bedrooms, and the house settled with a deeper silence, Priest and Septemus Hart glared at one another in the drab lamplight. The bodies around them were piled like cairns, the stink of them growing more fetid as the wind picked up and swept through the house.

The orchard whistled and moaned. Suddenly Priest felt comfortable and tired and began to drift. He reached out and took a jug of wine, drank everything left in it as the liquid splashed down his collar and chest.

There are times when you want to do nothing more than to weep in the arms of an older man that you can pretend is your father. When the burdens and responsibilities of being an orphan can threaten to buckle your back and batter you to pieces.

Priest looked at the bruised and crusted face of Septemus Hart and attempted to shove aside his enmity, grudges, and jealousy, and almost felt himself float across the room and embrace the man in an effort to find a lasting peace. He closed his eyes and let the wine lighten his mind, but when he opened them again Septemus was fixing him with a penetrating gaze that cut through all his remorse and mourning.

"Braulio never sent those messages to Sarah," Priest said. "You did."

"She had no mind on what I was up to."

"And that's how you decide to use your own wife?"

"Don't talk that way to me, McClaren. I don't answer to you or anyone."

"But why?" Priest asked. "Why do it at all? Why involve yourself down here this way?"

"I got my reasons."

"I want to know them."

"To hell with what you want."

"Don't you have enough money?"

Septemus's features smoothed out and for a second he seemed filled with a kind of grace. "It isn't all about money, son. It's about making something where there was nothing before. Carving out a piece of history for yourself because you can, because it takes a certain kind of man with that resolve and determination." He drew a breath, the polish and kindness already beginning to fade. "There's wars being fought in this country every day. I want to see some of them win and others lose. I aim to help certain people get on their feet. This close to the border they can do me good. We got a lot to build."

"Sarah is pregnant."

"Don't you think I know that?"

"But still you involved her in this play. Used her against me like that."

"You're a fool, son. I can make use of fools. It's just the way of the world. You got a gripe with it, then stop acting so god-

damn stupid and crazy all the time. I considered that you might do something half-
smart in your life and steal the so-called
ransom cash, but the thought never so
much as crossed your mind, did it?"

So that was why the ransom was so low.
Septemus's greed nearly ruined his own
plan. He didn't want Lamarr and Priest
carrying more than twenty thousand just
in case they ran off with it. "I didn't come
here for pay. I came for Sarah."

"I know. That's why I played you the way
I did." He sounded a bit contrite, but still
unapologetic.

"Tell me. Do you love her?"

"You dare to ask me that? You've got to
get over your damn sniveling, boy."

"Do you love her?"

"Get out of my sight, McClaren."

Priest was out of the chair and the knife
was back in his hand, with Braulio's tacky
blood still gleaming on the blade as the
point pressed into the wrinkled, heavily
veined bulge of flesh under Septemus
Hart's left ear.

Do you even love her, Septemus?"

Lamarr stuck his heavy arm out in front
of Priest. He'd cut all the buckshot free
and bandaged himself. "Let me take care'a
Daddy."

"No."

"I got the greater cause."

"Maybe not anymore!"

"Your heart ain't no more broken now than it was the day he married Sarah."

"Don't presume too much!"

As much as Lamarr hated his father, he'd never kill him. There was too much inside him that would always need Septemus's love and would be forever waiting on that love.

"I ain't presumin' anything. We both got our misery to drag us through the night and into tomorrow."

Priest was nodding but not to anything Lamarr had said. He was agreeing with the child's voice telling him that Sarah would never forgive him if he plunged the knife into Septemus's heartless chest.

But Priest didn't much care because he might just do the same thing to her. For Braulio the murderer he had felt some pity, but now, for everybody else, he allowed himself only rancor. Sometimes you were saved by your hate, after your love failed you at every turn.

He slept in the orchard, where the large, misshapen fruit continued to fall around him through the night. In the morning, he heard them burying the dead among the trees.

Lamarr had packed up the horses. Septemus and Jowett sat eating breakfast and some of the vaqueros had started to repair and rebuild the house. They had settled into a brooding, grim, but diplomatic alliance, passing each other coffee and sausages, flapjacks, biscuits and syrup. Like two bitter brothers living under the same roof. They were free to go about their business now that Braulio was out of the way. Jowett's obvious pain didn't quite give Priest the gratification he'd been hoping for.

The plaza had been cleared of the corpses, the rubble, the knives gleaming in the dust, even the blood.

No matter what the hell happened to you, life moved on. He took one last look at the pueblo and saw the woman from the cantina walking toward him.

It could mean anything. Perhaps she had a machete or a pistol hidden in the folds of her skirt. He waited, swallowed, wondering if she was the one meant to finally do him in. To set free *una spectra* or add to the sadness she had named.

She watched him with that same grimace of compassion and irritation and stopped before him. It took a minute but she eventually reached up to stroke his cheek, then strolled away.

"You really do have shit luck with women," Lamarr said.

Two days later they found Burial Jones Clay murdered on the trail. He was naked and the burning sun, insects, and birds had already gotten to him. He'd been brained with a rock that still lay beside him, and he looked almost happy.

"Should'a got himself a fat wife and learned to farm like I told him." Lamarr took the fact that they'd given Burial a chance to redeem himself as an act of true piety. "He musta started runnin' the minute he left the cantina."

"Alone or with somebody he couldn't trust?"

"Boy like that can't trust nobody."

"No telltale signs in the dust."

"Could'a been anyone. Some folks is like that, drawin' ill will to 'em."

"Should we take him back, put him in a box?"

"No. Miz Utopia wanted him to be comfortable. I think he'll sleep just fine where he is."

Priest felt a twinge of regret again and wondered if he was getting too soft. You'd expect it to be the other way around, that he would've hardened up after his years as a drunk, that he'd be smarter now and more durable.

He thought about the mindful attitude Burial had shown back on the pueblo, and how he'd had the urge to warn them about Don Braulio. He should've had the time to finish turning all the way around and making good for his troubled past.

But like he had said to Burial, we don't choose our trials. And like Burial had acknowledged, we're the chosen.

When they hit town, Lamarr rode off toward his shack without a word, understanding that Priest couldn't go home just yet. He headed off in the direction of the Hart ranch.

The outcroppings of sandstone bluffs, where months earlier several wild hands working for Septemus had chased down Apache women, spun gold and fire across the sky as the sun began to set. Now that Apacheria was well past the age of Cochise, and the U.S. Army had decimated most of the renegade bucks, few of the Indians among such a broken people were willing to fight any more battles. Chicorah was one of them. In the shadow of the rez, Priest could sense his grandfather up there looking on, the mountain spirits all lying back, reserved and cold in their judgment.

He focused on the ornate wrought-iron gate that stood closed before the ranch. A couple of sentries spotted him and took positions atop the walls.

Priest drew to the gate and Merullo's grizzled face appeared on the other side, staring. "What do you want, McClaren?"

"I'm here to see Sarah."

"Mrs. Hart to you, friend, and she didn't tell me you'd be coming back."

"Go let her know I'm here."

Your past followed you into each new day, and the hours stacked up behind you like gravestones.

Merullo once again proved he was smarter than Cobb, the previous foreman, who'd asked Lamarr on the night of the raid, "How 'bout I just kill you dead on your horse, nigger?" and reached for his pistol. Merullo pursed his lips and his solemn eyes skittered back and forth in his head but he didn't cause any trouble.

Priest was almost hoping he wouldn't be allowed entry, that the choice would be taken from his hands. Merullo swung open the gate and sent two escorts to ride with Priest on toward the ranch.

When he saw the main house it reminded him so much of Braulio's replica that he wondered if he were damned to do everything over again today: toss the dynamite against the window, forgetting to shoot out the glass, throw the stick through the door. Today and tomorrow and for Christ knew how long, until he'd delivered himself of whatever sin it was he was being damned for. One of the men knocked, exchanged words with a servant. It took fifteen minutes but eventually he was told that he was welcome inside.

A Mexican handmaid, different from the one before, led him through the same corridors and out the back, where Sarah again stood in the gardened piazza, staring at the mountains. The moonlight drifted so low and bright that it layered a light coating of white against Sarah's black curls. From the back she looked very much like his mother.

She turned expectantly, wringing her hands, and said, "My husband? Is he home? Where is he?"

Priest didn't know what to say. One of them might truly be a ghost, but he wasn't sure it was him anymore. "Septemus is fine. He'll be home soon."

"Oh, thank God. And the madman who took him?"

He withdrew the perfectly balanced knife, held it out to her. "My sister said this is evil. She told me to throw it down a mine shaft and not look back."

"And so?"

"I killed him with it."

"The man who kidnapped my husband?"

"Yes. I stabbed him with his own blade. There are tribes that believe I'm doomed to carry his soul on my back for the rest of my life."

"Why are you telling me this? What has it got to do with anything?"

He wasn't certain, and said nothing. She didn't ask anything more—not if Lamarr was alive, or Jowett, or what it had been like to drive into Mexico among the starving peasants and fight against a people he had no quarrel with, only because she had asked him to do so.

"Are ye angry with me, Priest McClaren?" She stepped close and her Irish scowl filled his vision, those dark, grave eyes full of competence and power, chin up. How he missed hearing her sing on the stage.

He stared at her and thought of the baby inside her. There would soon be another child in the world, and it wouldn't be his.

"You're pregnant," he said, or thought he said. The sentence came out so rough that it didn't make any sense. He repeated himself. "You're . . ." The words straying free, wayward, as if said by somebody else standing far behind him. "You're pregnant."

"Yes, that's true. Who told you?"

"Jowett."

Of course that would fill the last missing piece of her life for her. Now she had all she could ever want, and none of it came from him. He felt himself fading right before her eyes, as if he did not exist and never truly had. Their dead child called him Daddy and he went to his knees.

Either she knew the truth and had used Priest in the service of her husband, or she was ignorant of the man she'd married and didn't want to know the truth. She had to suspect, though, the way anybody who had run across Septemus Hart could sense the selfishness and greed and dissoluteness. Priest couldn't quite decide if she had willingly sent him toward his death or had merely manipulated him in an effort to save what she actually loved.

He saw the lamplight reflecting against the far wall and realized he was wandering into the glimmer of the blade. Her eyes widened in fear, and for the first time, despite all their history and beautiful hours, which confined his pain and gave it some meaning, he hated her.

"Are ye going to scar me, Priest Mc-Claren?"

"I ought to cut your throat!"

"I'll not argue."

Her face was wet but those eyes were dry. It took him a second to realize he was crying and sweating so furiously that he'd cast a sheen on her.

"Do you know what you did to me?"

"I had no choice!"

"Like hell!"

"I never meant for ye to be hurt. Yer the only one who could've saved him. You and Lamarr. The two of ye would bring him back alive no matter what yer feelings might be. Don't you see?"

"There was a time you'd never put me in harm's way. Now you use my emotions against me and set me up to face the devil."

The woman he'd loved so much, who'd once carried their child. What might've happened if she'd managed to bring the baby to full term? Would he be happy now? Would he be lying in bed beside her, listening to the child breathe in the cradle beside their bed, instead of hearing only the tiny voice in his head?

What had he done to bring himself to this?

Priest took a step back and Sarah came

forward, arms opened as if to enfold him in all his own fear. The same way Braulio had done as he died. Priest shouldered her away.

Maybe it was the *Ga'ns* spirits within him, or his grandfather's madness, or his mother's mute influence, but when Priest spoke again his voice was so calm and unfamiliar it chilled him.

"You got what you wanted, Sarah. Your man will soon be back home with you even though he's not worth an ounce of spit. You sent me off to die for him and I nearly did. You played your string out and won in the end. Now stay the hell away from me for good. We cross paths again . . ."

"And what then, Priest McClaren? Speak yer heart. And what will happen then?"

"Good-bye, Sarah."

The child cried for its parents. The weeping filled him, growing more severe until it was his own, and the tears spread out over his face and struck his lips. Something loosened and broke apart inside his chest and his fever for life began to burn again. The child whispered for him to ride away fast and not look back, so he did.

The salt dried on his face in the brilliant luster of the night sky.

Chapter Fifteen

Molly was holding Katie out on the porch as the traffic went by on Broad Street, rocking her and singing one of Lamarr's mother's songs to her. The livery sheds were alive with action, and it sounded like two drunks were trying to get on horses that weren't theirs to take. The wide shadows between buildings swarmed across the walkways. Carousing from nearby barrooms could be heard.

He sat on the top step of the porch, near her feet. Prickly pear blossoms wafted into his face. She reached down and touched his shoulder. He could still make out the bright red of her burned cheeks even in the dim lamplight falling through the doorway. She saw his face and the baby started crying, and Molly passed Katie over.

Priest held Katie close and she stopped acting up within seconds, the cheerfulness suddenly back in her now, those tiny fists patting against his chin.

"Didn't exactly go the way you were expecting, did it?" Molly asked.

"No," he said.

The wooden wind chimes rang together with a sweeter sound than the metallic tinkling of church bells or knives. Katie gurgled in Priest's arms and he drew her up a little tighter. The drunks from the livery were being chased up the block.

She waited about as long as she could. "What happened?"

"You were right about everything, right down the line."

"Sarah?"

"That, too. Clear as ears on a mule to anybody with eyes."

Molly winced. "I'm sorry."

"Don't be. The excursion taught me a few lessons."

"For instance?"

"That Lamarr and I have similar weaknesses in our character, which drive us to do stupid things. When there's a choice to be made, I have to go my own way, right or wrong."

"And did you? Out there on the pueblo?"

He'd been thinking about it for four days

302

and still wasn't sure. "I tried my best to do what was right. I'm just not certain I ever did manage it."

"What matters most is that you made the effort."

"I wish I could believe that."

He looked at her then and was surprised to see she was smiling, the way their mother used to do when she was proud. It made him grin, seeing Molly like that, and before he could stop it, he felt himself lifting a little, the black sorrow parting for an instant. That almost scared him, the fact that he couldn't even put his faith in the permanence of his pain anymore.

Katie was at the stage where she was beginning to let out brief hiccups of spooky laughter. She made a sound and he pressed his forehead to hers, let her hands tug at his hair for a while.

Family still counted. Blood mattered. He'd let his duty slide for a long time but he resolved never to let it slip by again. He might not have a baby of his own, but he had a niece who someday might need to count on him. He had to ready himself. There was still a hell of a lot of work to do.

"Gramps come back yet?"

"No, but I got wind that Chicorah was gonna bring him back into town any day now. Probably tonight, the way I figure."

303

"Starting to scare the Apache kids?"

"You know how it is. Even when he's Apache he still has nightmares in English, starts screaming about Grandma, all those fevers in his head leaking out. Nobody can get any sleep on the rez."

"It's a full moon."

"I saw. For some reason it shakes him up some, gives him bad dreams. They'll want to get rid of him tonight. Go wait for Chicorah at the edge of town. He'll be along soon."

Priest rode out and waited for less than an hour before he heard the stamp of two horses coming down the street in the darkness, and the murmurs of Gramps as the old man pleaded and tried to persuade Chicorah in his own tongue. You could tell he was getting white again by all the complaining he was doing, instead of accepting his fate and assenting to it. Gramps wore his usual grimace and his Apache was speckled with English words here and there.

Chicorah was alone and kept up his expressionless mask, but Gramps glowered, starting to sulk, becoming whiter by the minute. He wore only a breechcloth and his thin, loose-skinned chest was covered with white thatches of hair. He stank of mescal and he was shivering.

He glanced at Priest and the grief and remorse flooded into his face from every wrinkle. Every now and again Gramps's mind cleared enough to where he saw himself from the outside, his senses clear. It's the only time that Priest felt real sadness for the old man.

The son of sub-chief Sondeyka almost never traveled alone, especially in town where there were men who might fire on any Apache for jumping the rez. It meant he had something important and private to say.

Priest reached up and took his grandfather's hand, and the instant the old man touched him he passed out and slumped in Priest's arms. Was it relief or anguish that had brought him to this?

"You could have come to me," Chicorah said. His English had improved a great deal in the last year, and Priest wondered if he was learning it from Gramps, who talked in his sleep.

"I know."

"You are not my brother, but in some ways—"

"I thank you for the sentiment. But you once told me I had my own fate to find. I suppose I'm trying to do just that."

"But you took the big black."

"We went to save his father. It was his fate to go, too."

"Next time, perhaps our path will be shared."

"Maybe it will at that."

Gramps cried out, *"Ethel, Ethel,"* and Priest hushed him, placed his palm to the grizzled neck while the old man called for his dead wife. Was it going to be like this forty years from now? Priest running around naked and wailing Sarah's name?

He chewed his tongue until blood slid down his throat. When Priest looked back, Chicorah was gone.

Lamarr lay resting in one of the coffins again, maybe thinking of the Ohio Valley and running toward the Canadian paradise, or maybe how he helped his little daddy to swig wine, Septemus cooing and sighing like a baby.

"This really is comfortable. I could get used to this."

"You will one day," Priest said.

"Jesus ain't gonna call on somebody this beautiful for a long while yet."

"Don't throw heaven a dare like that."

Priest smoothed his plane over the wood, letting the repetitive action work into his muscles and level out his mind. He burned over whether leaving Septemus alive had been right or wrong. He realized he'd never find an answer to most of what troubled him, but he'd find a way to live with it.

For now.

An evil time would come again—soon, he thought, probably sooner than he could guess—and he'd have to finally go his own way.

"You're vexed with me, ain't you?" Lamarr asked, propping himself up a little like a dead man who isn't quite ready to go yet.

"Yep."

"'Cause I stopped you from killin' Septemus."

"Yep."

"I didn't do it because he's my daddy."

"You sure about that?"

"And I didn't do it because of Sarah, neither."

Priest felt the rage inside him like an animal ready to tear itself free. He had to reconcile with it, learn to discipline it. "Why then?"

"'Cause it would've been wrong."

"What's that now?"

"It wouldn't have been right, the way it was. Him unarmed, a tired, beaten old man in a chair, too weak to even run. You wouldn't have been able to forgive yourself afterward."

"I might've made peace."

"You ain't done so yet, not even over Yuma Dean. Nor that damn Preacher Deed, neither. You gotta clear your soul some."

"And how do I do that?"

"I don't know. But killin' Septemus would've taken you one step further away. That's for sure."

The next few hours passed in silence while he dwelled on it. The child whispered and gave him a few other thoughts as well, things that might remedy a few of his ills.

Lamarr appeared to be sleeping heavily, his dreams possibly filled with visions of his own dying, the pretty girls with tears in their big, beautiful eyes, sweat gleaming on all that nice golden brown skin, holding out armfuls of roses and daisies.

"I need your help," Priest said and Lamarr stood and got out of the coffin.

"For what?"

"Start lining all the boxes up."

"You got twenty, thirty of them here. What are you goin' to do now?"

He remembered Padre Villejo's poorly crafted lectern with the splitting slats, the rickety fence of chicken-wire surrounding the small graveyard, the nuns with the broken hoe handles, and the padre crutching himself toward the open doorway of his church as the dust blew in across the rotted floor boards. Molly still needed some furniture for the house, a crib for the baby.

Priest started taking the coffin apart, figuring he could put the wood to better use.

THE BIG FIFTY

JOHNNY D. BOGGS

Young Coady McIlvain spends his days reading about the heroic exploits of the legendary heroes of the West, especially the glorious Buffalo Bill Cody. The harsh reality of frontier life in Kansas becomes brutally clear to Coady, however, when his father is scalped and he is taken prisoner by Comanches. When he is finally able to escape, Coady finds himself with a buffalo sharpshooter who he imagines is the living embodiment of his hero, Buffalo Bill. But real life is seldom like a dime novel, and Fate has more hard lessons in store for Coady—if he can stay alive to learn them.